To Denise Grace

Sincerely,
[signature]

9-10-16

I WANT MY MOMMY

A Parent's Guide to Child Care and Education

Cameron Kidston

I Want My Mommy
A Parent's Guide to Child Care and Education

iUniverse books may be ordered through booksellers or by contacting:

iUniverse
1663 Liberty Drive
Bloomington, IN 47403
www.iuniverse.com
1-800-Authors (1-800-288-4677)

ISBN: 978-1-4502-7082-3 (sc)
ISBN: 978-1-4502-7086-1 (hc)
ISBN: 978-1-4502-7085-4 (e)

Library of Congress Control Number: 2010916421

Print information available on the last page.

iUniverse rev. date: 07/05/2016

This book is dedicated to my sons.
Both endured, learned and survived.

With special thanks to Author Barbara Seaman.
Ms. Seaman gave me the faith to continue on this
challenging path to write and publish this book.

Contents

INTRODUCTION

I Want My Mommy: A Parent's Guide to Child Care and Education tackles an extremely complicated and important issue that is explained in simple terminology and honesty. Primarily parents are told what choices are available in relationship to parenting and in the child day care and educational industry.

I am a parent, a teacher and a former proprietor of a regulated child day care center with at–risk children. At the opposite end of the industry's spectrum, I was a team teacher at a high–end licensed child day care center and preschool.

My formal education includes enrollment in five diverse school districts in three states in the Northeastern U. S. I have studied art in Greece, worked in child care in Italy and was trained in corporate business management in Puerto Rico. My first introduction to formal education was through the Reggio Emilia approach in the state of New Jersey.

As a parent and teacher I incorporated John Holt's method of teaching that supports the belief that children are naturally curious and eager to learn.

Additionally, I accumulated fifteen years of certification through The State University of New York–Early Childhood Education & Training Program, New York State Department of Health, New York State Office of Children and Family Services and Social Services; and the United States Department of Agriculture. The accrued certification supports behaviorism, human development, nutrition, discipline, safety, early childhood education and business operations in regulatory child day care centers, preschools, early childhood programs and schools.

I Want My Mommy incorporates a range of first account experiences from children, parents, teachers, directors, government regulators and civil servants in four states throughout the Northeastern U.S. The title of this parent's guide is based on what I have heard and other educators continue to hear while working in child day care centers and preschools across the U. S. and around the world.

Learning starts at the time of birth and this establishes the beginning for both children and parents. The chapters unfold unassumingly with a holiday in May for recognition of the profession of educators and caregivers in the U.S. and other countries. The unregulated and regulated child day care industry is addressed in a comprehensible manner and makes clear why the former is illegal.

Detailed explanation is given on the subject matter of the rate system which is nationwide and has a different hourly rate for the first six hours depending on the child day care center and whether enrollment is government subsidized or privately paid. The most important questions are covered as to what a parent should ask and expect when interviewing at a child day care center. Note: the parent is not interviewing for a babysitter.

Though a state standard for education may be a good idea, it is not feasible to implement and enforce these guidelines into the vast network of early childhood education, child care facilities and schools. This stark reality also applies to civil servants and under color of law employees who maintain a massive government employment link into the child industry from the moment of birth.

The chapter on food explains the federal government guidelines under the Child and Adult Care Food Program (CACFP). Food signifies different things to different parents and to the U.S. government regulatory system.

It may be true that when paying for child day care tuition you usually get what you pay for. However, it is by no means a guarantee for a higher quality of service. The reader is taken into the low–end and the high–end market of regulated child day care centers and preschools to understand the environmental differences.

Parents should be familiarized with the law in correlation to all regulated child day care centers and schools. Clarification is given as to what a licensor and their responsibilities are when employed to oversee regulated child day care centers.

My Family Day Care (FDC) covers a span of over a decade while working with underprivileged children in the inner–city. A Federal Law— Family Educational Rights and Privacy Act (FERPA)—is brought into play when a state agency crosses into another administration's jurisdiction while implementing a new state regulation.

Child care terms are reviewed, though the general U.S. population has a bad habit of lumping most of them under the title of Nanny. The last chapter addresses the term school that has become a catch–all phrase used by parents indiscriminately when talking to their children about child day care centers, early childhood programs and so on.

I am a strong advocate of Maslow's Hierarchy of Needs and Erikson's Psychosocial Development Theory. The educational curriculums that I created were swayed heavily by Carl Jung despite the fact that Sigmund Freud is relied on by Erickson's theory of stages. References are made throughout the chapters to both Maslow and Erikson in discussing implementation of new state education standards.

We as a society and globally come together collectively to participate in a learning experience and to co–create an inherent need to consciously be aware. This guide is intended to teach parents to choose responsibly and wisely in terms of birth, child care and education for their children.

This topic is brought to the public in a format that has never addressed these important issues as one. The goal on this occasion is to open and look behind the many closed doors.

Part 1
WHAT YOU SHOULD KNOW

Mother And Child Bonding

Open Your Mind

Immediately after birth, most but by no means all, mothers experience a surge of affection that is followed by a feeling that the baby belongs to them. The relationship between mother and child may develop gradually and strengthen over time. Occurring during this same time period the newborn brain is developing very rapidly for the first two to three years of life.

Early neglect is all too often the precursor of later neglect. When the child remains subjected to deprivation, inadequate or insensitive care, lack of affection, and low–levels of stimulation or poor education over long periods, later adjustment is likely to be severely compromised.

It is true that the mother and infant bonding experience may not occur at all or be delayed under certain conditions. Trauma during childbirth overpowers the natural surge for the mother and child to bond. Both verbal and physical violence interferes, slows down and may stop labor and the birth process altogether.

Under these traumatic circumstances, oxygen deprivation for the newborn will occur while in the birth canal. Sometimes this will result in serious neurological damage. The most prevalent effect will be physical and emotional trauma to both the newborn and mother. Sometimes evidence can be confirmed in the afterbirth that will reveal a hemorrhaged placenta. Additionally, meconium most likely will be present in the discharge fluid.

In theory, the increased contact at any time during the first days after birth produces a long–term improvement in the quality of the relationship between mother and child. Increased contact may in part make up for the marked deprivation that is a part of current routines in modern hospitals in the U. S.

It is said that with additional deprivation of insufficient contact, this may have serious consequences for the child. Both child abuse and failure to thrive without organic cause are found more frequently in infants who have been separated from their parents immediately after birth. One of the problems in the later development of children who experience early institutionalization or significant neglect is that there may have been no opportunities for the caretaker and the infant to establish strong and mutual attachments in a reciprocating relationship.

Over the past decades a grassroots movement supporting natural childbirth has emerged in limited ebbs and flows within the U. S. The continuing goal is to help with the bonding, awareness and adjustment process of being a parent. One of the key factors in supporting this goal is preventing the violent behavior and dominating controls during labor and childbirth.

Becoming a parent can be a time to powerfully build one's intuitive skills. Some believe that on a spiritual level, souls are being united or re–united and awareness helps the parent to be in touch with one another, spiritually enhancing one's ability to listen to the child's needs. Others believe physiology is the strongest determining factor that unites mothers with their newborns.

Prevalent in the U. S. and other global cultures is a definition that requires women to suppress or devalue their own female nature. To recognize her full self in relation to the archetypal feminine is a transition of enormous proportions. The woman is returning to an affirmation of the primordial feminine. She is the banished and the one expelled from a culture that she was born and raised into.

The gift is the full range of the woman's instinctual nature that includes the energetic force of her individuality, her strengths, innate intelligence and the connection to cyclic time and nature in all things. Unless that link is consciously retrieved women wander half alive. All feminine elements are innately supported by nature and earthly instincts. This represents an extreme opposite to a polarized masculine consciousness ideology and cultural environment.

Open Your Eyes

For more information on childbirth Naomi Wolf's *Misconceptions: Truth, Lies, & The Unexpected On the Journey to Motherhood,* was released in September 2001. The book's framework is about the birthing practices in America. The reading is particularly for those not familiar with the workings of the hospital birthing industry, the questionable medical interventions and the possibilities of natural birth and midwifery.

Additionally, the DVD *The Business of Being Born,* was released in 2007 by director Abby Epstein and produced by Ricki Lake. The documentary takes a hard look at America's maternity care system and the different outcomes.

I observed along with other women health care providers the epidemic of violence that is acceptable and practiced on women in childbirth. When confronted, the behavior of the hospital directors, and the OB/GYN Chief of Staff—who trained the physicians—their reaction was to deny and conceal the routine violent behavior. For decades the physicians and other staff had set into place, management systems and controls that enabled these types of practices in the labor and delivery rooms.

Thought provoking would be if those who participated in these wrongful acts would allow that type of violence to be used on their wives and daughters. What would possess doctors and other medical staff to use violent behavior against women during the time of labor and giving birth? The answer to this question directly goes back to the teachers—OB/GYN Chiefs of Staff, universities and hospitals who educate doctors and others that these types of practices against women are allowed and it is incorrigible in the hushed controlled birthing industry.

On one day a small group of women picketed outside a hospital and the affiliated clinics that were under the U.S. Federal Grant—Maternal Infant Care Program (MIC). The group of women knew that the doctors at the participating hospitals had repeatedly mistreated them during labor and delivery. The women's numerous efforts were noble and courageous. They knew right from wrong and they spoke up.

For these few women they believed that their mistreatment they had experienced was due to their race. What the women did not know was that MIC had contracted with an OB/GYN Chief of Staff whose duties were to hire, train, and supervise the doctors, hospitals and clinics. This doctor was hired as an educator for the new generations of doctors. Race had no boundaries as to who would experience the worst of the widespread violent behavior in the labor and delivery rooms. These women were medically and socially expendable. The OB/GYN was taught this behavior by his teachers and colleagues and possibly his father, it is learned behavior and it did not originate in the hospital environment. Rather it came from their roots and was incorporated and accepted treatment towards women in labor and birth in a hospital setting. The OB/GYN Chief of Staff repeated the cycle of this type of violent obstetric care in his teaching of interns while acting as director for the MIC program.

The women's picketing had absolutely no effect on the problems that were occurring behind closed doors. When approached, other women in the community would not or could not talk about the matter. Either they did not recognize that the violent behavior against women under these conditions was wrong or they found the subject matter too private in nature to discuss.

A woman police officer assigned to the sex offense squad (SOS) alleged that when a woman was in labor and delivery a doctor could do anything they wanted to do to her. Women had no rights under these circumstances, "the doctor was in charge and he could to do whatever he wanted to do". The woman police officer repeated these words over and over as if she were dumbfounded by the question. Who were her educators that trained this female police officer assigned with special training in assault?

The hospital was made aware of the doctor's teaching and practice methods. The board of directors of the hospital knew that there would be no consequences for him or them to be concerned about. The doctor had a relative holding a key position for decades at the state department of health agency, their sole job duties were to oversee and conduct local investigations of public complaints. The intricately intertwined government monies, government held positions, an OB/GYN Chief of Staff who was contracted with the MIC program and others, ultimately resulted with each person to look the other way on this matter of public concern.

At the same time in the geographic region there was one of the highest infant mortality rates in the U. S. A special investigative panel and task force was created by the government to investigate the problem. The government's inquiry on this issue of public concern was an accumulation of deliberate indifference in health care services and violent behavior on the issue. Subsequently the matter became buried and hidden away as it always had been.

One of the persons named on the investigative task committee was the OB/GYN Chief of Staff who was contracted with the MIC program. Others on the task force included the doctor's colleagues and the hospital where he was employed. These same individuals had prevented nurses, midwifes and other women to be heard on the customary violent behavior and other abuses directed towards women in labor and birth that had been occurring at these facilities for decades.

Most of the nurse–midwifes had experienced a politically controlled business monopoly in the health care industry that had shut them out. The OB/GYN Chief of Staff informed one chief nurse–midwife that it would take time for change. She waited. The nurse–midwife believed everything he told her which in the end turned out to be a calculated deception on his part. The manipulation and the violent behavior continued. The nurse–midwife grew old and subsequently entered into a meditation retreat while going on a long sabbatical.

Maybe the birthing industry in this country is a commodity that is impervious. Some women are brainwashed and don't know right from wrong or are indifferent on this subject matter. While others do care and know violent behavior towards women in labor and birth is wrong, these women are silenced by the birthing industry that is bigger than they are.

Open Your Heart

When a woman has a supportive natural nonviolent birth experience, planted is the seed for the mother to bond healthy and strongly with her infant. This birth experience does not guarantee all mothers will maternally bond with their children nor have any maternal instincts form into the mother child bonding process.

Going against the natural birth process would be the physically aggressive and verbally violent, highly controlled or negative childbirth experience. In negative settings, the mother and infant bonding process will be repressed, negated or denigrated.

For a select small number of women, who do experience a violent or negative childbirth experience, they will take extra measures into their own right in the caring of their infant in order to compensate for the obstruction of the one–on–one bonding. One alternative choice is to have as much contact as possible with their child by nursing, holding or nurturing even though it most likely will be a highly sensitive, demanding and an exhausting job.

In one case a new mother who I interviewed in my child day care, took these similar instinctual therapeutic steps after her experience. The new mother and her husband knew the foundation for damage in the mother and child bonding process had been laid. In these instances, for these rare women to make their own directive, an autonomous timeliness is required to heal the wounds. There also comes a need to create an attitude of reverence and an honoring of sacred feminine values.

The new mother established a routine with her husband. He acted as her support system to allow as much as possible time for the mother to hold, nurse and physically touch the newborn baby. He supported her in the decision for her not to return to her former job after her unexpected negative birth experience. In this case the mother's autonomous time line began from the moment the newborn arrived and continued months later when I met with her.

Childbirth lends support to feminine consciousness of women's instincts and feelings. It is meant as a sense of dignified self–respect. Connection to the feminine offers a new old archetypal pattern of identity. A woman whose identity takes her back to the feminine base as the orienting pattern of her ego sees life very differently from women grounded in the patriarchal culture model for her sex.

The archetypal feminine in matrifocal cultures holds and honors women in their female body and its potential for the cycles of the natural world. In contrast the patrifocal cultures holds dominance over nature and man's ego over the all. This led to the patriarchal attitude of privilege, mastery and conquest and this is what gained dominance in our cultural history.

The divinity of the archetypal feminine, trans-personal psyche layers, the source of innate feminine divinity and instinctual wisdom has been severed from contemporary feminine consciousness or awareness in the U. S. and globally.

A Profession

Give Acknowledgment

Provider Appreciation Day (PAD) is a special day to recognize child care providers, teachers and other educators of young children everywhere. Started in 1996 by a group of volunteers in New Jersey, PAD is appropriately celebrated each year on the Friday before Mother's Day. The founding organizers saw the need to recognize the efforts of the tireless providers who care for children of working parents.[1]

The child care profession is one of the most underpaid occupations in this country, and yet early childhood is the most critical developmental period for all children. The early childhood profession not only plays a critical role in supporting healthy families and children but is also a key part of our entire national economy.

These insights have been repeated by verbatim by various government agencies, non–profit organizations, private and public institutions and grass roots movements involved in the early childhood education industry. These words have been used and overused so many times for so long by so many people that they have lost their meaning on the whole.

It is important that parents understand this profession and what is involved in the care and education of young children. The number one complaint heard from individuals who work in the regulated child day care business and with certified school teachers—is the parents. This is not to say there are no other criticisms and problems in the early childhood education and child care industry.

---

[1]   Reprinted with permission from, National Association of Child Care Resource & Referral Agencies (NACCRRA) and Child Care Aware. http://www.NACCRRA.org/.

Many parents lack the comprehension that the profession does not equate to being babysitters for their children, this attitude is an ongoing cultural and social problem passed on by generations. Additionally, child care providers, teachers and educators are not in a professional capacity to raise children for parents.

An increasingly high number of parents do not or cannot parent their children. Parenting includes a full range of responsibilities from the simplest task of feeding their child a meal to issues dealing with child behaviorism, discipline and development. This common problematic issue crosses over into all socio–economic groups of parents.

Non–parenting extends itself from the two parent professional working household to the struggling single parent living below the U.S. poverty level. It has become commonplace in the profession to witness some parents to have no real interest in their children. Parents and children live separate daily lives. The children are not a number one priority in the parent's lives but are more geared as a financial responsibility.

One cause out of many for this prevalent and current problem is the continually broken cycle of physiological parental bonding that parents perpetuate by not interacting or spending time with their children. Another term that may be used to describe the latter is personal bonding. This becomes null and void by child and parent separation over long periods of time.

Individuals who work with young children in regulated child day cares have been struggling for years to convince the public that they are not babysitters. What is generally perceived by most parents is to not identify the legitimacy of professional child care providers as child care and early childhood teachers. It is accepted and common knowledge among people who work in this profession that a supportive and nurturing educational environment for a young child, in or out of the home, is critical for the child's future development and wellbeing.

The new job title introduced for regulated child day care workers is, 'Early Care and Education Specialists'. The Early Care and Education Specialists provide the custodial care and needs of young children along with their early educational developmental needs. The new professional job description introduced to the public was meant to separate and legitimatize regulated child day care as a profession yet was never embraced by the mainstream U.S. public.

As a proprietor of a regulated child day care center for over a decade, most parents who had children enrolled in my center could not comprehend what regulated child day care entailed. Child day care centers and early childhood program directors would often recount to me similar encounters with parents and non–parents alike. The condescending and degrading comments were endless, from both men and women, in relation to the profession and the services being provided. The words used reverberated back to the term babysitter or being defined as doing nothing all day while being paid for it. This mindset continues today, and included in this maligned group of working professionals are certified teachers who teach young grade school age children.

These prejudicial ways of thinking, currently come from young adults passed on to them by older generations. Both generations think nothing of voicing openly their brash personal opinions to teachers and directors. For the people in the profession who encounter these never–ending disparaging remarks, they cannot envision where this way of thinking has come from or when will it stop.

Today these heated debates on the matter of professional work identity in the regulated child day care and early childhood education industry continues. It results in directors vehemently denying that they are babysitters to adults that challenge them on what they do for a profession and living. It continues up the ranks throughout the early childhood education system while educators are constantly confronted with professional work identity.

It was a bigger dilemma in my child day care when dealing with parents of at–risk children. I wrote a definition and description of what a regulated child day care was required to implement according to state regulations. I included a descriptive outline of state licensing requirements regarding early childhood care and educational study that are mandatory fields for all state licensing for centers, whether the teacher has a college degree, state certification, neither or both.

When this approach did not change the parent's way of thinking, an amendment was written under a policy section in the parent contract outlining the rules for the parent's expected conduct while inside my child day care. I would later discover that other child day care centers found it necessary to implement this information into their parent and center contracts in an attempt to continue educating the public on the regulated profession.

Meet My Educators

Three out of five public school districts that I was enrolled in used progressive teaching methods. Two public school districts in two states did not. Teaching techniques ranged from the Reggio Emilia Approach, Independent Study Programs for College Preparatory, mandatory student (ages 12–18) teaching programs and optional student teaching (ages 13–14) at an annexed elementary school on a suburban school campus.

At the age of 5–years–old I was enrolled in a school that exclusively used art to teach young children reading, writing and arithmetic. The use of simple art technique applied design with natural materials found from nature. Learning through art formulated the process of thought for applying aesthetics, asymmetric, symmetric and linear patterns fixated within interpretation of all things. I would not be who I am today without the use of art in that format in my own education at an early age.

In another state the local district's high school taught with no classroom walls. As an alternative the classrooms were open and designed similar to cubes. The course study offered consisted of college preparatory programs that included optional independent study courses in the arts. The teaching curriculum was strongly based on the humanities. This method of teaching philosophy teaches students to think and to take responsibility for their own learning. It gives them the tools to teach themselves and others. This state standard for education and teaching philosophy was applied at three out of five school districts that I was enrolled in.

One out of three high schools in two states offered independent study courses under the supervision of a teacher that the student would meet once a week. This approach to teaching included no peer groups, no classroom, no attendance, no competition and no testing. It was one–on–one teaching. The assignments were given, performed independently within a given time frame and then evaluated by the teacher before progressing onto the next assignment.

For twenty–years I have taught children of all ages, including school age children, while creating and applying college preparatory level curriculum for children of all ages up to 18–years–old.

Without the specific foundation in education that was experienced as a child, I would not have the ability to deconstruct education and use the application in real life challenges. Childhood educational experiences help formulate who we are and how we think.

Be Realistic

When some parents drop–off their children in the morning at child day care centers or early childhood programs they arrive and depart with the false impression that their child is the only child in the room and center. It is not uncommon that parent's believe that they have hired a service that caters to their child in accordance to the parent's wishes on any given day.

Identical to schools, all regulated child day cares have a scheduled program and a curriculum that all children as a group follow throughout the day and the week. Sometimes in unusual circumstances a child may be split from the others and be given free play or assigned an individual task to do on their own. This situation depends on the child day care center or preschool and is designed for the child who cannot cope making it through the day within the schematics of the group, whether it is the classroom or the whole school. Not always, but usually it is behavioral related that consequently effects the other children and the teacher's ability to teach.

A regulated child day care center or school is not a babysitting service. The child care educator or teacher is not going to take instructions from a parent on what they expect from the teacher in relation with their child on an individual basis.

Find out the Essentials

Some children enrolled in child day care centers, from an early age, are developmentally delayed later on due to the fact that the parents have minimal interaction and engagement in learning activities or experiences with their child. It is defined as environmental developmental delay. This may also be seen in some orphanages and other facilities that house large volumes of abandoned children.

On one occasion at a child day care center, a parent and teacher conference was held. The teacher and director suggested to the parent to do certain activities at home with her child. The parent told the director that she did not have the time to do the activities. She also said it was the child day care center's job and not hers to do. The parent told the director she was not going to listen to what they had to say and left the room. This type of parental thinking and behavior is not isolated to this specific case.

Almost all parents seem to have an idyllic vision of their children enrolled in child day care centers and preschools. Child day care centers' protocols are explained to the parent before enrollment; the schedule, the program, and curriculum for all the children in the group. Too many parents do not comprehend the reality of how child day care centers are set up. The program starts from the beginning of the day at the time of drop–off and continues throughout the day until the time at pick–up. There is very little room for individuality or alone time for the child.

Aggression from children and teachers is unavoidable, regardless of the center being exclusively private or a high volume government subsidized facility. The percentage of violence is different from center to center. It is a reality that accompanies volume control and a hierarchy within large groups of children and adults placed together in large facilities for extended periods of time.

On one occasion at a center a 3–year–old child took a solid wooden chair, lifted it and purposely smashed the other child on his head. All it takes is one violent child to cause irreparable damage to the other children. Imagine more than one child injuring other children and attacking teachers on a daily basis.

This violent behavior defines a hostile and aggressive environment. If it occurred in any other work place or in a private family home it would result in serious legal ramifications. Violence is a byproduct in the child care and education industry and it is not isolated to a few individual centers or schools.

It would be self–deprecating for a director or principal to inform parents of the level of violence that occurs at their child day care center or school. Some parents believe aggressive behavior is normal and a rite of passage for children in a social group environment. Many parents accept violent behavior as part of the emotional development for early childhood or school age education. They believe their child will gain social experiences and survival skills when placed in groups with other children.

Add the Numbers

In my child day care program, I would not accept enrollment of more than five children at one time. My state registration allowed my business to accept up to eight children under the state regulations for full capacity enrollment.

As sole proprietor I received a negative response across the board from both educated and uneducated parents. They all wanted their personal fantasy fulfilled. The irony was that it was an identical fantasy all of the parents shared in their way of thinking. They wanted their children to socialize with a certain volume of other children their own age or older throughout the daytime. This belief system was so strong with all of these parents that they applied their personal desire for children as young as infants and toddlers to play and socialize in their own age group. It is a nightmare and not a fantasy for children.

Parents should spend a day or two in child day care centers' baby and toddler rooms. The crying, high level of noise and stress, random acts of violence from one or more children on another child is what occurs when volumes of children are grouped together for hours at a time. In the 3–year–old and 4–year–old toddler rooms it differs very little from the other age group rooms.

At a teacher and parent night meeting at a high–end center, the teachers in the 2–year–old toddler room showed a video to the parents of their children's activities taken over a month's time. A few parents mentioned that they thought it was wonderful how the children played so nicely together without fighting or crying. The teacher very subtly mentioned to the parents that any negative behavior from the children had been edited out of the video. The number one priority when a center or school facility is at full capacity is volume control and managing the children to get through the day. When there are too many children and too many teachers in the child day care center and early childhood programs or schools, stress is extremely elevated and contagious communicable diseases are very high.

Many teachers' pay is low and some have no health insurance. Tuition is high and the child day care center's perfect image conveys trust for the parents and this is what parents want and buy into. The high–end child day care center and early childhood programs or schools, may or may not, offer a higher quality of child care and education then most available.

Behavioral problems accompanied by violence most likely will always be prevalent and that alters the time, energy and stress level at each facility. This also determines the outcome for what was or was not accomplished in accordance to the teaching curriculum or program for that day.

As in any profession, some teachers excel in their work, some are standard and others have no right of being in the business. It is not a difference in job title alone but a difference in experience, education, training, job performance and salary while functioning within state regulatory systems. These are the variables that define educators not as babysitters.

REGULATED CHILD DAY CARE

Stop the Infighting

An annual state conference for educators was designed for nursery school teachers, licensed child day care providers, pre–k school teachers and other early childhood educators working in the profession. In one workshop geared for reducing the risk of child abuse and false allegations in early childhood programs, the presenter was a chief state licensor from a neighboring state. He made the statement, "you know that nursery schools and child day care centers do the same thing." The nursery school teachers in the classroom piped up in unison, "no, that is not true, not in this state, we are different."

They had missed the point that the instructor was making. He knew that as an out–of–state guest at the state conference it was best to move on than to debate with a growingly hostile faction. He quickly and quietly changed the subject and went on with the class instruction.

This type of bickering boils down to various accreditations and credentials held by different early childhood education facilities and educators. Regulated child day care centers started out as the tortoises in the early childhood education industry. Other early childhood education programs, both government and private facilities, decades ago were the hares in the early childhood education industry.

While the latter distanced their professional identity from all child day care centers, some regulated centers caught up and surpassed the hares. Additionally, early childhood education accreditation organizations began to include regulated child day care centers in their accreditation process and award system equal to pre–k, kindergartens and other preschool programs.

Some state educational training and workshops that were specifically funded and approved by the state for regulated child day care centers, were sometimes teaching cutting edge information in education. In many cases the conferences and workshops surpassed the education and training that the licensed school teacher with a Bachelor's or Master's Degree in Early Childhood Education or other field of study had received in the past or present.

In some instances, in–house center training from licensed teachers and directors employed in centers was repetitive of what they had learned from a long–time ago. Or the training was part of the center's personal signature making the instruction being taught inaccurate. This type of system for in–house staff education is commonplace in order to meet state mandatory training for the high volume of the center's staff while they simultaneously receive paid training for attendance. This type of training saves on time and money in the child education industry.

Educational Conferences and workshop classes that I attended under mandatory training for the CACFP were different and advanced compared to in–house CACFP training at two different centers in another state and in this state. In one example a lead teacher at a center with an Associate Degree and a lead teacher with a Master's Degree in Early Childhood Education and Development—one had little and one had no CACFP training—each violated CACFP policies at their respective licensed centers while employed as full time teachers.

Currently in the early childhood education and care industry, a center may or may not include the title early childhood program. This is the old terminology that schools usually like to use. What parents need to know is *it mandatory for all regulated child day care centers to provide an early childhood education program.*

Particular accreditation does not guarantee that the standard for education and child care is greater than the non–accredited. The term school does not guarantee that the education and child care being provided is greater than the child care center. The pre–k and kindergarten's early childhood program is not a guarantee that they are providing a greater education program then the child day care center. Each individual child care center and school provides a different result and standard for education in early childhood development and child care.

All state licensed schools for school–age children provide different methods, styles and qualities of education, yet under state education law it is mandatory for all licensed schools to follow the same curriculum and regulations. The same rules apply to all early childhood education and child care facilities.

There will always be numerous variables in every educational facility combined with the application of the government's internal organization of a system. The outcome will always produce diversity in children's education and child care where no two centers or schools are the same.

There are now both hares and tortoises individually fighting for a position in the vast network of the early childhood education and child care market place. It may be difficult for the uneducated consumer to distinguish who is who. This includes preschools, nursery schools, government and private early childhood programs, government subsidized or private regulated child day care centers and public, chartered or private schools.

Ask to see and read the facility's program not their accreditations. State licensing or registration is a must. Accreditations may be a good way to approximate the educational and child care services being provided. However, accreditations may be deceptive and are also known for sometimes hiding behind in any competitive marketplace where the bottom line is to generate a highly successful and financially profitable business.

Catch-Up with the Times

Once during an interview for enrollment in my child day care, a college professor for women studies defended babysitters across the world and told me there was nothing wrong being a babysitter. She was looking for child care for her infant and asked me questions from her long handwritten list that was tailored for a babysitter and not a for a regulated child day care center.

One of the questions that she asked: "do you smoke in the home" I reminded the new mother that she was interviewing a state regulated child day care and smoking was illegal in all regulated child day care centers. She asked me the name of the last book I had read on child care. I referred her to the two classes that I had attended the previous month. The classes were underwritten by the state bureau of early childhood education and I paid the tuition fee. The workshops were designed for the emotional development of the young child and re-framing discipline to encourage positive emotional development. I discussed with this new mother the subjects on child development, behaviorism, teaching methods for early childhood, the child day care center business, my program, policies and the state regulations for all child day care centers.

State regulation sheets for regulated child day care centers are available from individual states to anyone who requests them. In this mother's mindset she was looking for a babysitter while interviewing at a state regulated child day care. She had set expectations of what regulated child day care was and did not have the capacity to move beyond her preconceived ideas.

At a state government sponsored class designed to implicate a new state standard for education in centers and schools, the instructor referred to an incident at the center where she had been the director. A teacher at the end of the day at the center was putting make–up on her teenage daughter. The director fired the child day care center employee on the spot for not paying attention to the last two remaining children who were waiting for pick–up from their parents.

Any form of child care or education entails a very high responsibility and demands the adult's full attention at all times. This consists of a continuous tuning into the children to effectively provide supervision and interaction on a one–on–one basis which allows for ensuring the safety and welfare for children in their environment. Being highly intuitive, consciously aware and sensitive allows some teachers to work on a higher level with children than probably most professionals in the field. It is a type of language translation unfamiliar to the majority of adults. It is time consuming, difficult and is involved work that is personally rewarding. For other types of educators, at the minimum, they are required to pay attention at all times to all of the children in their care and environment.

With most parents and educators, what is expected and accepted as normal behavior from the adults who provide the education and care of children, greatly differs from center to center, school to school, neighborhood to neighborhood and family to family.

I witnessed in an inner–city neighborhood both government early childhood program facility's employees and a government subsidized center's staff, doing what the children's parents accept and how they act around their children. Each day that I walked by two playgrounds, all of the employees were either on their cell phones, smoking cigarettes or conjugated in groups socializing. The children were in clusters on the other side of the playground or on asphalt playing with no adults close at hand to supervise them. There was no one–on–one relationship or direct supervision or interaction with the children from the attending adults.

This sort of accepted adult practice by teachers, child care workers or parents, creates a void where there is no adult guidance or nurturing. The question becomes who is raising the children?

Pay–Up or Be Terminated

With many of the parents, when it came to pay my child day care center for overtime or the government subsidized mandatory co–payments, the parents debated with me on why they should not pay. They told me that I did nothing while being paid to do nothing. In all of these cases that I experienced the parents were the ones who actually did nothing with their children while at home. Please refer back to environmental developmental delay mentioned in the chapter, "A Profession" with the subheading, "Find out the Essentials."

These parents of at–risk children received government subsidized child day care from county and state programs while attending adult educational programs or working at low paying jobs or attending court ordered medical counseling and etc. The government's market rate for payments is an average of forty–percent to sixty–percent less than private child day care market rates. The common thinking of parents—I don't want to pay or I won't pay—played out in other child day care centers as well with both private and government subsidized payees.

In all private child day care centers the contract requires the parents to make a two week deposit in order to protect the centers from parental non–payment of services while under contract. In the centers that contract with government subsidized parents there is no deposit or protection for these centers from parental non–payment of services. Centers may request deposits from these parents who are low–income and who receive government entitlements. The norm is that it is unrealistic to expect a two week deposit from parents who live below the poverty level.

The parents who complain or refuse to pay for child care justify their behavior on the premise that child care services of any kind should be a free parental entitlement in this country. My own conversations with private paying and government subsidized parents became too familiar in similarity. Parents consistently considered the job as women's work and devalued the profession.

On the issue of costs, most all of the parents wanted the service to be free. The prevailing argument of these parents, which still exists today, is why should the mother or father work at a paying job if part or a large portion of their wages pay for child day care services?

There is a correlation between a mother who takes care and teaches her child while not generating an income. Our society devalues those that care for children in general. In other words, why pay for it, if it was free before? It was always an unpaid job to be a full–time mother.

Add into the social equation that children's enrollment into schools in the U.S. has been provided free by the government since legislation was passed in the late nineteenth century. Ultimately through the centuries many parents used the government's educational system as free child care while they went to work or attended to other daily tasks. That is the origin of the U.S. government school system.

At a high–end child day care center the parents paid one of the highest private market rates for an eight hour full–time day. They were willing to pay extra whenever their needs increased. Some parents voiced their appreciation and were in awe as to how the center's teachers had the aptitude to be with their children for eight hours a day. The parents admitted openly how they found it sometimes overwhelming to care and spend time with their children for long periods of time.

The obvious answer to the parent's difficulty is an ironic one. The more time parents leave their children to be cared for and taught with other adults, the less bonding occurs between the parents and their children. At the end of the day as the years pass, children and parents may become virtual strangers to each other.

Find the Parent in Yourself

There are ramifications for leaving a child almost ninety–percent of their waking hours five days a week in a group environment with numerous adults and with high volumes of transient children. This is the lowest end of available regulated child day care. For many parents they have the false impression that their child goes to an endless child's like party at the child day care center and are learning social skills and playing among their peers.

The effects of leaving a child with a babysitter or unregulated child day care are not particularly encouraging. The term babysitter is the definition that too many government civil servants think and say when referring to any child care that the government approves for subsidized payments. I would hear this inaccurate terminology used for more than a decade by county civil servants, state workfare and low–income parents when addressing regulated child day care centers.

There is an endless continuation of re–education programs and advancements made in the child care and education industry by non–profit and government sponsored educational organizations aimed to re–educate the public about regulated child day care centers.

Parents pass on to others their own misinterpretations of their preconceived ideas of what regulated child day care centers are and do. These inaccurate definitions range from addressing a regulated child day care center as babysitting or going to school. Some of these parents, who cannot or do not parent, are third and fourth generations of government recipients for institutional subsidized child care, early childhood programs and other educational programs. Private payee parents also misuse terminology when referring to child day care centers and early childhood programs. Many of these parents were not raised by a full–time mother or parent but by other caregivers. Their behavior and thinking is multi-generational with cultural and economic influences accumulated over the decades. Presently and parallel to the past, parents and the individuals working in the profession are on a two way street. This predicament is not going to change anytime soon.

Mammals have a natural born ability to parent from the time of birth. What if this natural cycle from the time of birth is broken in humans and replaced over repeated generations by an alternate man-made system. Will this natural born ability become dormant and neutralized?

This is one reason out of many that there was a soaring division between exclusively private child day care centers and early childhood programs versus government subsidized child day care centers and Head Start. The former is now catching up to the latter with the phenomenon of non–parenting.

In an interview a government subsidized parent was looking for a child day care center to provide eleven hours of child care for her 3–year–old child. This child had spent her entire life since 6–weeks–old in numerous government contracted child day care centers. Her enrollment included two meals and two snacks a day. I point this case out because it must be said that numerous government subsidized child day care centers and informal caregivers had fed, cared and raised this child since the age of 6–weeks–old for intervals of eleven plus hours.

What emotional, psychological and developmental learning disabilities will this child face in the future as she matures? Will she have learned simple living skills? When this child becomes a mother will she have the natural ability to bond or parent with her own child? Will she parent as her mother had done before her and her mother's mother? Will the next generation she creates be raised by institutions and underage relatives as her mother had done with her? Will her human female psyche be too fractured to make healthy choices about her own reproduction and parenting choices?

The government's subsidized payment for contracted child day care centers averaged twenty–percent more than the government's subsidized payments for contracted family and group child day care. These rates allocated by the government fueled the myth among the uneducated that family child day care cost less and are not equal in educational standards to child day care center facilities or early childhood programs.

Additionally, the government's rates paid across the board for all subsidized child day care centers decreases according to the increase of the age of the child. This price reduction creates a false belief in many parents that in general child day care centers have less work responsibilities with a toddler than an infant. I have heard this often incorrect ideology from parents with at–risk children.

The truth is that a mother or other adult caring and interacting one–on–one with an infant or toddler creates the growth of connecting neuron pathways in the brain and this determines the developmental growth of the child. The degree of responsibility of child care does not equate to changing a diaper opposed to the child using a toilet or being spoon fed versus the child feeding them self.

Some small exclusively private family child day care centers' rates are consistently equal or higher than the private rates for high–end child day care centers. It comes down to adding numbers and overhead costs.

Private paying and well educated parents seem to be the only people privy to the fact that in general, some small and exclusively private family child day cares often have a higher level of quality child care and education. In a private family child day care there are a smaller number of children, one–on–one nurturing and attention, a home environment, less spread of contagious diseases, fewer incidences of problems with transition throughout the day, less turnover of educators providing the child care and so on.

For example, at an exclusively private family child day care, the proprietor accepted no more than five children full–time. One day a two and a half year old child picked up a child's plastic chair and threw it at her. She called the parents and informed the mother that her child's enrollment was terminated, as of that day, due to his violent behavior towards her and around the other children. Termination was nonnegotiable.

On another occasion she had accepted enrollment of a newborn. At two weeks into enrollment she informed the parents that she was terminating the contract of the infant due to the fact the infant wanted to be held for most of the eight hours.

The eight hours was equivalent to her child care center's full–time hours of operation. When she was not holding the infant, the newborn would cry and it was compromising her quality of work with the other children. The tuition rates were equal to the highest full time rate of an exclusively private child day care center facility.

This family child day care had a waiting list for enrollment that exceeded one year. This proprietor followed her own business principles by only allowing a small number of children for enrollment. Her business thrived and she was well compensated in her profession and the parents adhered to the child day care rules. Termination was nonnegotiable. The parents trusted and respected her. This case represents a healthy, strong good marriage between a high–end exclusively private family child care in a well educated high–income neighborhood.

Violent behavior at this family child day care from a child towards an adult or other child was met with zero tolerance and resulted in immediate termination. This type of action forced the parent to look at themselves, take accountability for their child and not place that responsibility on the child day care or educator. She also recognized that a baby needs to be held when they cry and in this case the baby needed more care than she could provide. Intelligence and responsibility, trust and zero tolerance for violence are traits that she was allowed to maintain in her business while being paid a professional high income. This case is very rare to find in the industry and the only one I have encountered.

Ratio of children and adults in child day care center facilities is much higher than a group or family child day care center. Add to this scenario all of the children in the large group are the same age in a large room for up to eleven hour days in a center facility with multiple rooms of hundreds of young children and adults. Some of the children will come and go throughout the day and others will stay the full eleven hours.

Some private child day care centers are open for eleven hours a day with parents leaving their children at the center for ten hours on average. Sometimes these are franchises with high tuition rates and the parents consist of two working professionals who require child care for long hours and can afford the rates. Child care center employees will change throughout the day.

This is also commonplace for government subsidized contracted child day care centers for workfare parents and low–income eligible parents some of whom work two jobs. The government subsidized parent payments for eleven hours of child care are an average rate of forty–eight percent less than what an exclusively private child day care center would be paid by a private payee.

The government subsidized day care centers are open two or three hours or more a day on average than what the accepted norm for full–time enrollment is for smaller volume child day care centers in the private sector. The ineffective low–end government subsidized child day care system was created out of a high demand with the beginning of the shift in the child care industry under the new government policy of welfare to workfare decades ago. Adding to this mix were the high numbers of single parents who were and continue to raise children on their own while working one or more jobs because they do not receive adequate financial and child care support from the other parent. Some states do not have government subsidized child day care and parents are on their own as to where and with whom their children will be cared for and educated while they are at work.

The question is what will happen to these multi-generations of children who spend most of their lives from the time of infancy being institutionalized in large groups, with many caregivers and with other emotionally detached children. Are these children taught and raised not to feel? If they are taught not to feel, then they are not capable of empathy.

Without empathy their consciousness level is nonexistent or limited and violence, learning disabilities, aggression and bullying will be permanent markers for these children's psyche as they mature into this country's next generations and enter into the workforce. This is not to say that children who are not enrolled into institutionalized child care are exempt from learning these unnatural negative behavioral qualities. They too are susceptible to becoming emotionally deprived.

The government subsidized contracted child day care centers also enroll children from the private sector. The private rate of tuition is equal to the government rates or may be based on the parent's income. Stipulations in a government subsidized child day care center's contract allows for the center to charge private payees more but they are not allowed to charge less than the government's subsidized rate.

Some high volume government subsidized contracted centers are similar to puppy mills. The business scheme is to have the lowest overhead cost with the highest volume of enrolled children. Parents, children and workers are transitory. Government payments are the lowest on the market, full–time hours are the highest on the market and there is a cash flow that is usually not readily available and delayed in–transit from government funds. The revenue barely turns a profit for the one at the top who is the director, proprietor, or maybe the owner of a franchised child day care center.

Some exclusively private child day care centers and preschools have been found to have faults of their own with controversial ideologies on discipline, teaching methods and with the care of infants and young children. While some centers are in high demand and have waiting lists for enrollment, full capacity enrollment in centers and schools may be red flags to the educated consumer.

High enrollment numbers ultimately challenge daily volume control of the children. Numbers have a significant role in the industry and parents should be aware of how they affect the quality of child care and education for their children.

RATES

Don't Crash the System

When I reviewed the child day care center's business rates with the professor who taught women's studies, she could not understand the rating system. She debated with me as I explained the universal tuition rating system under government regulation for child day care centers. She said the tuition rating system was unfair to her and that she did not want to pay it based on the full–time or part–time regulatory tuition rates. It was ironic how the conversation had turned, a woman professor who was consistently contradicting her field of teaching.

The regulated child day care centers' rating system is not up for debate with a child care center's director. It is nonnegotiable. The tuition rating system in the U. S. for children's enrollment into regulated child day care centers is comparable to tuition rates for nursery school enrollment. Tuition is not an hourly babysitting rate when a parent needs child care.

Some, but very few regulated child day care centers do accept drop–in children when space is available. The hourly rate for this specific service is the highest on the market and it is very difficult to find regulated child day care centers that accept drop–in children on demand. A state license or registration allows a certain number of slots in the child day care center to be filled, a drop–in is like a wild card, and it is inconsistent and unpredictable for business.

When all of the full–time and part–time slots are filled, it is illegal and highly irresponsible to accept on demand drop–in children. It also violates a regulated child day care center's insurance policy coverage. Insurance coverage is mandatory for most state regulated child day care centers.

The tuition rate system for regulated child day care centers has two daily rates either part–time or full–time. The part–time rate is hourly up to six hours and the full–time rate is based on six hours and up. Full–time may include up to eleven hours that a state regulation outlines as the maximum hours allowed under full–time definition. Different states may differ on state regulation for maximum hours allowed under full–time definition.

Certain child day care centers may not accept enrollment for any child that exceeds eight hours or more. By definition of state regulations for child day care centers eight hours would fall under a full–time rate. For example, a parent is not permitted to a credit of three more hours that they think they are entitled to because under state regulations the cap for full–time enrollment is eleven hours. This type of thinking goes back to parents believing that they have a special entitlement to free child care and want as many hours as possible under paid tuition enrollment for their child. These types of parenting cases include both government subsidized and private tuition payees who inevitably want to leave their child in the centers for as many hours that they can without paying.

In rare cases some child day care centers operate and run on twelve hour shifts with a high volume of children and employees. Remember that a state law defines full–time maximum hours allowed for a child in a regulated child day care center as eleven hours. This does not mean the child day care center's operating hours are by law a maximum of eleven, it actually means no individual child may be enrolled in a regulated child day care center for more than eleven hours in one day.

Learn Your Numbers

Depending on the child day care center that you are interviewing with, the full–time number of hours allowed under their policy differs from each child day care center. A rule of thumb is the less hours a child day care center is open, it is better for quality control for the child, the parent and educator.

A full–day rate in my business included six to nine hours of child care. More than nine hours would be considered overtime in the parent day care center contract. At a high–end day care center the facility was open as a whole for a maximum of ten hours a day. No individual classroom was open for ten hours. No child was enrolled for more than eight hours unless special arrangements were made before hand, and they paid an extra fee.

Individual class rooms were open five to nine hours per day, depending on which class or age group the child was enrolled in. Most of the parents were working professionals or stay–at–home parents. At this specific center when the parents could not pick–up their children at the designated time, they paid fines and overtime. A classroom in rare cases may be open for nine hours when there was a demand but the full–time rate was for eight hours. In this example the policies for part–time and full–time enrollment for tuition rates meet government regulations under the rating system for child day care centers.

Be On Time

Most child day care center employees and other educators frown heavily upon parents who leave their children in a child day care center for long extended hours and especially when the parent picks up their child at the last minute during closing. This rule applies to dropping off the child earlier than scheduled, even when it equals minutes. Don't drop–off early and don't pick–up late without prior approval. Adhere to the rules or the parent will be fined and charged.

A child day care center will have many different shift workers coming and going taking care of the child depending on the hours needed by the parent. The teacher with whom you drop your child off with in the morning at the center, most likely will not be the same person that you will meet at the end of the day at pick–up when the center is open for more than eight hours.

Parents will pay additional fees for late pick–ups and the employee will be paid overtime. This does not compensate for the inconvenience of the exhausted teacher or the director who has to stay late to lock the doors while waiting until the last child leaves the premises. In most cases if the parent drops off early or picks up late outside the contracted hours or operating business hours there will be a fine plus a steep overtime charge.

At a hospital campus child day care center-under the government's Business Credit Tax for Employer Provider Child Day Care Facilities-the center's policy was if the parent picked their child up one minute late after six p.m. the parent would be fined and charged overtime. The child day care center effectively enforced the one minute late pick–up policy. The parents learned quickly to adhere to the center's rules because fines and fees were nonnegotiable and were implemented swiftly when a parent broke the rules.

Go Find the Money

Child day care center rates do differ. There is a variety of payment arrangements and this can include private scholarship awards or a third–party government payee on behalf of low–income parents. The parents may be required to pay a co–payment to the child day care center based on their income and number of family members living in the household. Some states do not have government subsidized child day care programs. Do your homework on your own state.

A private family child day care may have the same rate as the high–end exclusively private child day care center. A group or family child day care or child day care center located in a rural area may have the same rate as the government contracted rate that is the lowest rate on the market. Location of child day care centers influences the rates in the area but is not the determining factor.

Some child day care centers charge different rates to different parents according to their income or number of children from the same family enrolled in the child day care center and some do not. A private child day care center usually does not accept or may limit a very small number of government third–party payees. Private centers may have a lower rate than the highest rate on the market and yet will not accept any government third–party payees.

As mentioned previously, when the federal and state governments changed welfare to workfare it produced a huge shift in the child day care market regarding rates and hours. This gigantic wave created an enormous divide between the private child day care sectors and government subsidized or government contracted child day care centers.

Become an Educated Consumer

There is a black–market child care industry. Black–market babysitters work out of their homes, are unregulated and do not follow the state regulations or laws for child care. Additionally, they work in homes for families well under the minimum wage and off the books.

In general, the black–market babysitters in homes consist of usually undereducated, untrained individuals without a background check, reliable references or credentials. They will charge well below the average rate in the child care industry. The lowest rate in the regulated market is the government subsidized rates.

A parent who had hired a black–market babysitter paid a rate equal to the highest rate charged by a private high–end center. The parents did not understand the standard rating system for regulated child day care centers in the U.S. The parents were paying an hourly rate for nine hours that would have equaled the same full–time rate for an exclusively private regulated center. Naively the parents made a decision based on what the new mother's sister, a registered nurse, had chosen to do and what her other female relatives had done before her for many years.

This particular black–market babysitter exceeded the number capacity allowed for the age groups of children permitted for a legal regulated child day care center. The total number of children in her care, regardless of age, exceeded capacity allowed for a regulated child day care center for teacher to child ratio guidelines. She also violated state laws for the number of children allowed in her home to babysit that were unrelated to her. She was a babysitter and not an early childhood educator operating a regulated child day care center.

More than three years later I ran into the parent. She told me that she had enrolled her child into a private child day care center that was a preschool because child day care in the home was not educationally oriented. The parents mistakenly believed their child was enrolled into a preschool receiving an education. Actually the child was enrolled into a regulated child day care center facility. Previously the parents mistakenly had believed that their child had been enrolled into a child day care. In actuality, previously the child was in a home with a large group of children being babysat by an unqualified black–market babysitter.

When I met the child she was 3 going on 4-years-old, she screamed sporadically, cried consistently and threw tantrums throughout the day in the child day care center. The teachers reassured the parent that things were okay with the child's behavior. This daily violent behavior affected the other children in the room and was mimicked.

The mother was a consultant and worked for a large business firm. When it came to being a mother and understanding child care and education, her preconceived ideas created an obstacle in her ability to learn beyond what the women for generations in her family had been taught.

Licensed and registered regulated child day care centers whether in a home or facility follow the same government regulations, codes and laws and all require a program, daily schedule and curriculum to be followed for every age group.

The business records are kept daily in all regulated child day care centers and record keeping is mandatory under state regulations. The records are made available for government inspection on demand. When in doubt check with your individual state government's child day care regulations.

Whether the parent is low, middle or high–income and paying for legal child day care they may be able to reduce their taxes by claiming the credit for child and dependent care expenses on their federal income tax return. In general, but not always, this tax credit does not benefit the low–income parent whose child day care costs are mostly subsidized by a government child care assistance program and the parents are making very low co–payments to the child day care center.

When a parent chooses black–market child care under the pretense that they are receiving a cost–effective deal, they will not be able to take this tax credit.

Avoid the Backlash

Some family and group child day care centers have no shift employees or breaks for up to nine to eleven hours. They cannot afford to pay another employee or find someone part–time that is willing to work for such low wages. When this challenge occurs it is usually the proprietor of the child day care center working without breaks.

At the other end of the spectrum, the underpaid employees in child day care centers may encounter developmentally behind or behaviorally problematic children, absent parents, uneducated or overworked co–workers and under-staffing. The high volume of underprivileged children and their parents are using the government subsidized child day care centers and early childhood programs to their breaking point. Both parents and government planners will get in return a new type of human exploitation in children and teachers.

The results are also overused and underpaid child day care center employees which usually in most cases means a high transition of workers, burn out and low morale. The violence that children experience who come out of these facilities is real and under reported. The parents that I spoke with accepted it as the social norm for children being children. Taking the high volume of violence factor into account, provided will be the lowest quality of services provided under government subsidized child care and education. The parents of the children I met had the misconception that they were sending their children to school and would repeatedly tell their children school would make them smart.

The early childhood programs and regulated child day care centers are challenged daily by parents. Parents are responsible to care, teach and raise their children. Educational goals are sidelined as children's first needs are not met at home before arriving at child care centers and schools. Learning requires that children be fed, well rested and not be distracted with violence and other behavioral issues on a daily basis. Ultimately this challenge has become a vicious circle in this type of environment that can result in no more than warehousing very young children in large groups.

This fact reflects that children are not spending their time in a stable home environment with their parents. The mother or father have the title of parent but do not parent or raise their children. This leads a child to experience a form of severe parent rejection during a very vulnerable early young age. What are the lasting repercussions for these children?

See and Learn

The government's stand on state regulated child day care centers versus the black–market child care industry came full circle in a complete bureaucratic contradiction with new child care reforms to accommodate workfare and low-income parents. Under a state law illegal child care is a person who baby–sits more than three hours at a time for more than two children that are not related to the adult who is doing the babysitting.

The state law was established to promote professionally trained licensed regulated child day care in the state and to curb the burgeoning black–market of unqualified caregivers and unregulated babysitters. More than two decades ago the average black–market rate for child care was fifty to sixty–five dollars a week equaling forty plus hours for one child. Today the private rate for enrollment in a high–end regulated child day care center can exceed three–hundred fifty–dollars a week plus the cost of incidentals for an average enrollment of 40–45 hours per week.

In the past decade the government decided to make subsidized payments to informal babysitters to baby–sit workfare or low–income children at a lower government rate than what is paid for enrollment into a regulated child day care center. An informal babysitter can be a relative, sibling or friend or an acquaintance that baby–sits. They receive payments from the government for the workfare or low–income working parent who cannot find available regulated child day care that will accept subsidized government payments.

Some states do not provide subsidized child day care payments for workfare or low–income parents. Many parents persistently place advertisements for hiring babysitters to come to their home to provide child care at a rate of $5 an hour while the parent is at work or at school. This type of hiring practice and rate is illegal and violates labor laws and child care regulations. Check with your own state that you live in for your state's labor regulations regarding babysitting in the home.

For every step forward the regulated child day care profession has taken, the government policies to accommodate workfare and low–income parents have taken child care backwards. It is ironic that the informal baby-sitter's rate paid by the government is less than the average rate paid to black–market babysitters by parents.

In one case a parent on workfare discovered it was impossible to find regulated child day care for the night-shift she was forced to work while she was on the government's mandatory workfare program. In the regulated child day care center industry, the cost of insurance and liability alone for nighttime child care outweighs any government contracted income for the center.

Workfare ordered the single mother back to work when the youngest child was 6–months–old and her oldest was 2–years–old. She could not find government subsidized regulated child day care for the hours that she was required to work. The government agency approved payment eligibility for informal child care for her two children.

The mother was required to work at a fast food restaurant that was part of the government's Work Opportunity Tax Credit Program. The fast food restaurant received federal subsidies to create low paying, low skilled, short term jobs for the poor. One of the largest targeted groups were single mothers on welfare.

The government paid the informal child care rate to the father's new girlfriend for babysitting the two children. The children slept at his home while the girlfriend spent the night.

When the youngest child was 18–months–old the mother found a new daytime job and enrolled the two children into my child day care through the government's subsidized low–income eligible child care program. When it was time for the parent to fill out the application to receive approved government paid child care, there were two sections: informal child care babysitters or formal child care licensed child day cares.

The mother concluded that I was an informal babysitter because I was working in a home. I had previously explained in the interview process what a regulated child day care center was and what I did in my program.

Since her ex–boyfriend and his girlfriend had babysat her children in a home she thought by definition that I must be an informal child care babysitter. The mother enrolled her children into my child day care while she worked during the day.

When the mother was a child her mother had lived on the streets. She had been raised by her grandparents. As she grew older she also lived on the streets and that is where she met the father of her children.

After three months of enrollment in my child day care, one night the mother put her two children to bed, waiting until the oldest was asleep, she went back to the streets and left the children home alone.

In the aftermath the custody of the children was given to the father. He had no actual parenting skills. His mother had left his father and him when he was 5–years–old. At the age of five he was sent outside by his father to play, and he was told: "you can do anything you want to do but don't get into trouble" right before his father shut the door.

In some instances, the parent will have the government pay their mother or grandmother for informal child care who in return may give the money back to the parent who is in financial need. Other government subsidized options available are to have a sibling baby–sit the children and the government would make payments to the child in charge.

This brings back the universal question concerning children raising children. Who is raising the children being paid by the government to raise their siblings?

Sick Days

Plan Ahead

Terms of absenteeism are included and defined under individual child day care center policies. This differs in all child day care centers whether they are private or government contracted and subsidized. When a child is absent from the child day care center the parent is responsible to pay for the scheduled blocked time contracted between the parent and child day care center.

At some child day care centers there are exceptions to the rule. At a franchise center, their contract with the parent permitted the child six sick days every three months in which the parent did not have to pay for their child's absenteeism and the clause included vacation days. Any absenteeism over the allotted days, then the parent had to pay the child day care center for those absent days.

At this specific exclusively private child day care center they have a high volume of enrollment and one of the highest tuition rates on the market. The center can afford to not have the parent pay for the child's absent sick days. The center has this policy to encourage the parents not to bring their children to their facility when the child is sick to avoid spreading communicable diseases. This is the exception not the norm for most child day care centers that include paid sick days in their contracts. Unfortunately, this does not stop the spread of communicable diseases, nor does it stop parents from not bringing their sick children to child day care centers.

Private family child day care centers are usually going to include in their absenteeism policy that any absent days are to be paid by the parent. The business revenue is too small to cover losses for nonpayment of sick days or vacation days.

Another example to look for is an absenteeism clause at some child day care centers that may include the parents to pay for the vacation time when the child day care center is closed. This usually would include no more than two weeks that the center would be closed.

In larger facilities, when they are closed for two weeks of vacation, there usually will be no charge to the parent. Government subsidized contracted child day care centers are paid for up to fifteen absent sick days over a three month period. Government subsidized non–contracted child day care centers will not be paid for the child's absent sick days.

The second biggest complaint from child day care centers and schools is regarding the parents who drop–off their sick children. Too often the parent knows their child is sick and contagious but unfortunately too many parents believe this is acceptable social behavior on their part because most everyone else does it.

A new government regulation required every regulated child day care program to establish a Health Care Plan. Individual child day care centers will have this policy included in their contract and this is a state regulation. Not all states have established the Health Care Plan regulation. Check your own individual state regulations for regulated child day care.

When I worked at a high–end center, a parent nonchalantly dropped off their child who was almost 3-years-old and had a broken leg with a cast up to her thigh. The parent brought the child without a doctor's note of approval for the child to attend the center. The teacher refused to take the child on the basis of the absent note from the physician. The parent then went to the center's director and had the teacher's decision overturned. The classroom of children spent a great deal of their day walking up and down the staircases from one room to another. The child with the broken leg had to be carried by the teacher throughout the day when changing rooms. She could not use the elevator with the child because the other children in the class would be left in violation of state regulations for teacher to child ratio guidelines. At the end of the day and while waiting for pick–up in the toddler gym, the child crawled on the carpeted floor with the motion and speed of a sloth as she dragged her heavy cast on her leg across the room. Another child with gleam in her eyes purposely tormented the child with a broken leg by sitting on her back so she would become totally immobile.

Each child day care center has different policies concerning sick children. Some centers accept children when they are sick or only accept children who are non–contagious. The list is long for what is acceptable and non–acceptable under the child day care center's Health Care Plan. Enforcing these individual Health Care Plans that affect all the children and staff is challenging for centers and schools.

The most common problem in all child day care centers is the crowd disease factor and the spread of contagions infecting children repeatedly at a very young age. Sometimes this leads to other physiological debilitations.

One parent I interviewed had removed her child from an exclusively private center after he had been enrolled in the center since the age of 6–weeks–old. He constantly became sick with continual ear infections and had multiple surgeries. He was almost 2–years–old when I met him. The interference with his hearing and multiple infections had delayed his developmental motor skills for walking and balancing. The mother had decided to remove the child from further enrollment in a large center facility environment. He was continuing to receive physical therapy out of his home. The mother was employed as a part–time government worker.

After dealing for years with many infectious communicable diseases in my child day care, I changed my health care plan to the Well Child Health Care Plan. This means acceptance of only healthy children into the child day care center would be permitted. I reviewed this policy with the parents. They continued to sneak their sick children into the child day care. Parents would rationalize that the child day care would take care of their child better than other people they knew or that it was not possible to find an alternative caregiver. Additionally, if they stayed home with their sick child they would not be paid for a missed day of work.

Some of these explanations may have been the same reasoning for the father who brought his daughter with a broken leg to the center. What would have been the outcome if the father had a broken leg, would he then have taken time off from his job and stayed home?

Take Responsibility

Many times a parent will not tell a child day care center that their child is sick because they cannot afford to miss work and would not be paid if they took a day off to care for their sick child.

At a center a teacher had sent a child home with a one-hundred-and-one temperature at four o'clock the previous day. The center's Health Care Plan stipulated that a twenty–four period was needed before the child could return to the child day care center when a child has a fever.

At eight–thirty the next morning the parent brought the child for drop–off much to the dismay of the teacher who reminded the parent about the center's Health Care Plan. The teacher told the parent she could not accept the child into the classroom. The parent in turn went to the director to argue his case of how he was in a hurry and had a business meeting in another city that morning. The director overturned the teacher's decision and the Health Care Plan, she allowed the child into the classroom.

This type of contradiction of written policies dis-empowers the teacher's role in the classroom, while undermining her professional capacity in her relationship with the parents and children. It also compromises the health and welfare of everyone in the child day care center or school.

In this same classroom on another day a parent pushed their child into the toddler room and made a quick dash out the door. As the child was eating her breakfast, eye contact was made with a teacher and it was obvious that the child had pink eye. The child was 4-years-old and said that she had allergies and that she was allergic to flowers. At the time it was winter and there were no flowers inside or outside. Had she been coached by the parent to make that statement about her eyes if when asked by a teacher at the center?

The child remained in the child day care center for the full day until the parent picked her up. The father took her to the doctor the next day. The doctor confirmed that she did have pink eye.

If a parent cannot respect their child enough to care for them at home when they are sick, at the very least they should consider the welfare of the other children and teachers in the child day care center. This rule of consciousness also applies to all school–age children in schools.

During the interview with the part–time government employee who was looking for a private family child day care, she complained about my Well Child Health Care Plan policy. The parent stated that if she did not go to work for the day and stayed home with her sick child she would not be paid for a sick day at her part–time government employment. My answer to her predicament was to find an alternative back–up plan for when the child does get sick.

More than once I encountered a parent in my child day care center that would not be aware that their child was sick during the first signs of infection. More often than not, the parent would deny that their child was sick. Was this behavior done consciously or subconsciously or was it plain non–parenting?

Some children in my child day care center, who were sick, showed little or no immediate symptoms as they had low–grade infections and were unsuspecting low–grade carriers. This condition is similar to many child day care employees and school teachers who have high immunity systems from years of exposure to communicable diseases.

My advice to all parents is to be prepared because your child will become sick during their enrollment in a child day care center. The same is said for older children enrolled in schools. Some child day care centers at the first sign of the child being sick will call the parents to tell them to pick–up their child immediately, it is nonnegotiable.

Interviewing

Do Your Homework

Usually what you pay for is what you get. Do not assume this is always true, as in any business it can go either way. The fact remains that most parents are not well informed but rather misinformed when it comes to early childhood education, including centers and schools. I am using the term center when referring to all three–types of regulated child day cares. It removes from the general public's confusion and misconception about regulated family and group child day cares in the U. S.

The media in the U.S. has been challenged in this area for years when reporting on the topic in the news. Currently the news media generally uses the term "child day care center" when referring to all three–types of regulated child day cares.

The three–types of regulated child day cares are listed as family, group and centers. There is a fourth type of child day care that goes through a process that requires that the programs achieve a nationally recognized system of accreditation. These types of accreditation processes are an opportunity for non–government organizations to conduct a thorough examination of every aspect of the early childhood program based on their accepted quality of standards. When the accreditation process is completed the center or school will publicize in their marketing the center's additional accreditation awarded to them. Examples of additional accreditation are the: National Association for The Education of Young Children (NAEYC), National Association for Family Child Care Accreditation (NAFCC) or other individual quality rating award systems.

Some non–government accreditation award programs have been awarded to government public schools. In one case an inner city public school had a sixty–percent low–income enrollment in their pre–k and kindergarten classes.

The public grade school had the option to receive grant money and additional services through a state government program if they applied for and were awarded NAEYC accreditation. At the high–end child day care center where I had worked they had obtained NAEYC accreditation.

The most important things you should look for in any regulated child day care center is their tuition rate, their program, the center's Mission Statement, how many children they accept for enrollment, teacher to child ratio guidelines and the center's policies in relationship to state regulations. The rule of thumb is less enrolled children in the class room and center is a better choice. These are the first and most important questions when interviewing for any regulated child day care center.

To determine the validity of any center's early childhood program the parent needs to review the program used at the center and not become solely dependent on additional accreditation that is being marketed to the parent.

The second set of questions should be about paid sick days, termination policies, medical and immunization requirements, paid vacation days, the amount of deposit required, what day is payment due, how many hours are included under the full–time rate, what is the part–time and full–time rate, do they accept overtime for prearranged late pick–up, what is the food policy, what is their Child Health Care Plan and so on.

The interviewing process is different at each child day care center. An interview may start over the phone or the Internet. The next step is to set up a face to face interview or there may not be an interview because neither the parent nor the child day care center matched each other's basic requirements.

Remember Nothing Stays the Same

The probability of changing policies, changing programs, changing state regulations in all regulated child day care centers will occur and this will indicate a change of the center's contract with the parents.

I met a husband and wife team who operated a private group child day care. Their center's contract was twenty–five pages long and required the signature of both parents. Some child day care centers do nothing more than have you sign a uniformed short page contract, a few other release forms, fill out a medical form signed by the doctor and make a deposit for child enrollment into their center.

At one private center the handbook consisted of twenty–eight pages and this did not include the ten or more forms needed to be filled out by the parents before enrollment. In this center the child and parents' personal files were held by the lead teachers in the center's classrooms. An additional copy was filed in the director's office. There was a high turnover of lead teachers.

Personal family information was available and made known to more than one person.

State regulations require that all child day care centers show the interviewing parents where their child will take their rest time. It was a common courtesy that most child day care centers included into their policy before the new state regulation was enacted. This new regulation was passed because some centers were not showing the parents where the children slept and some parents were not asking.

The tour and interview by the director or proprietor with the parents should be thorough. This entails an explanation of how each room or space is used for the center and where the children will spend their time throughout the day.

New state regulations incorporated that all children must wash their hands upon arrival at all centers. For most centers this was a common practice previous to the new state regulation and for some it was not.

When I worked in a high–end center the children and staff were required to wash their hands when entering each room. There were many rooms in the building. Like most child day care centers communicable diseases remained commonplace. Children and teachers washed their hands on an average of seven times or more a day. During my time teaching at the center I became infected with walking pneumonia. It is a common communicable sickness among young children. It is an experience I will never forget. I was fortunate enough at the time to have health insurance obtained prior to my employment at the center. Two months later I had no health insurance.

Unrealistic expectations are made from regulators and adults that the routine hand washing will curtail communicable diseases. At this center, children from ages 2 through 4-years-old, were under time restraints to process as quickly as a group of fifteen per room while washing their hands so they could move on with the daily program. Sometimes the soap or towel dispensers were not working at full capacity. The motion sensor faucet's water temperature came out cold and cooperation of the children to correctly wash their hands according to the established state regulation was a daily challenge.

This is the reality at a high–end child day care center. The actuality of enforcing the washing of hands regulation at low–end child day care centers is dubious. In one case at my center a three–year–old challenged me each morning on washing his hands at drop–off and told me that he had washed his hands at home.

Don't Panic

A parent that I knew called a child day care center to set up an interview. The center explained to her and to all potential interviewees that anytime was acceptable to schedule an interview as long as it did not coincide with the children's lunch time. The parent did not go through with the interview.

She was filled with apprehension because she was not allowed access to their center during a specific time. She came to the conclusion that this was a strategy to conceal something sinister that was transpiring at the child day care center. The ridiculous propaganda about child day care centers by the U.S. media was a strong contributing factor in her thinking process.

Parents should know that right before, during and after lunch in all regulated child day care centers it is the most demanding and hectic time out of the day. The children are very tired and hungry. They are going through multiple transitions. This time includes serving and feeding groups of children sometimes in consecutive shifts.

All staff is on hand and their first priority begins with food prep, cooking and gathering and prepping the children to wash their hands and sit for a meal that is served family style that adheres to CACFP guidelines. The next transitional phase is clearing the tables, washing their hands and taking the children for a bathroom break, washing their hands, gathering their sleep items before prepping them for rest time.

This all encompassing process is performed on a schedule every day and is monitored by center regulatory licensors and CACFP monitors with unannounced visits. Every day during the process record sheets are simultaneously being filled out.

All focus and priorities are on the enrolled children and there is no room for distractions that would compromise the safety and welfare of the children during scheduled meal times. A distraction would include conducting an interview at the center with a prospective parent and their child before or during meal time which converges on large groups of hungry and tired children while staff is in compliance with state and federal guidelines.

In my own center all interviews were conducted when there were no children present. On rare occasions I did interview during the children's scheduled rest time but this was an exception to my rule. In my center an interview would last one to two hours. A file would be given to the parent with my center's policies and contract. A sit down and review with the parent would follow. After that I would give a walk through. The interview concluded with questions and answers.

Encouragement was offered for the parents to ask any questions they wanted to ask without hesitation. The parent was given additional educational information on basic child care development and behaviorism including a copy of Maslow's Hierarchy of Needs, the Child and Dependant Care Tax Credit and more. My goal with parents was to not necessarily proposition them for their business but for the parent to walk away with more knowledge than with what they had walked in with.

A parent should accept this as not only the norm but expect it in making an educated consumer's decision on child care and education for their children

During the interview process for many of these parents they had preconceived ideas about the interview. It began with their misconceptions that they would meet the other enrolled children and then the group of children would go off into the distance to play while the interview was conducted by me. This consistent parental pattern of behavior and thinking was not isolated to any one socio–economic group of parents that I interviewed. I can only conclude that they came from previous generations of non–parenting and did not have the capacity to understand what a regulated center involved.

As stated in the earlier chapter the attending child caregiver or teacher has to have their full attention on all of the children all of the time, this does not equate to being physically present in the nearby vicinity to the children while conjugating with other adults.

At a high–end center the director interviewed both parents and the child. Interviews were continually conducted daily though there were no available openings. At the time of the walk through, the explanation of the offered programs and the center's Mission Statement were explained. The parents were given the option of being put on a waiting list. The parent's ability to meet the center's high tuition rate for the infant or child was not a guarantee for enrollment.

Ask Now

Who will actually be providing child care and teaching your child is an important question for the parent to ask. A sole proprietor of a regulated child day care center usually works directly with the children. Sometimes they may hire or use outside help or a substitute child day care employee to assist them in the daily operations.

In the case of child day care centers at a larger facility the directors and assistant directors will not be working with your children on a daily or part–time basis. They oversee the teachers and other staff. Their role is more administrative, sales and marketing. Some directors implement their own program and place their personal signature on what is acceptable and not acceptable for the care and teaching of infants and young children. This template is integrated with the individual teacher's personal signatures as to how the children in each class will be cared for and taught. Not only is this the format at early childhood education centers, it is the identical system for school-aged children attending schools across the U.S.

In the low–end centers there is a higher turnover rate of employees. This means during the enrollment of your child they will usually have many different caregivers and teachers that are transitory during their enrollment. This also occurred at a high–end center that I was employed at.

In group and family child day care centers it was discovered that friends, relatives and neighbors were being hired as substitutes or assistants. New state regulation was passed requiring mandatory registration of all substitute child day care assistants. Registration includes a state criminal background check for clearance and finger print registration. Under new state regulation, registering a substitute was mandatory even when that center did not employ one.

Each newly employed staff member in every regulated child day care center must fulfill the requirements of state clearance for criminal background checks and fingerprint registration. In a sole proprietor center the individual must go through the same process every two years upon renewing the child day care center's license or registration.

Don't Get Lost

An assistant director from a non–profit employer linked center told to me that her problems were not with the parents but with the staff workers. The center had a worker who had been employed for many years. The worker refused to follow the new program with the children. She arrived late to work many mornings and for numerous other reasons she should not have been working with the children at their center. After much documentation had been recorded on her job performance or lack of it, the staff member was terminated.

Within two months the center was forced to rehire her after the union fought her case and won. The assistant director explained to me that this was not the first challenging case within their unionized center. Three years later this child day care center closed operations due to escalating costs.

At a federal government employee child day care center all of the employees had to have no less than a bachelor degree to work in all positions at the center. Employment requirements were different at a high–end center. The center required a minimum of previous work related experience in the field or an associate degree with a major in any area of study. The new employees would be trained by the previously hired staff. Some of the staff had been employed for more than twenty years at the center. This type of hierarchy system certainly protected a few teachers who had seniority and lacked professionalism.

Some centers hired students from the community and state colleges who had no experience in childhood development and education but were planning on working towards a degree in that area of study. Sometimes employees were hired based on their college education though it did not relate to childhood development or education. This is a selling point that center directors make to parents—that for the most part their employees hold a college degree or are working towards one.

The question should be where, when and what did they graduate in? This may mean a Bachelor's Degree in History received thirty years ago. It also can mean a young student enrolled in the local community college who switched their area of study away from early childhood development and education because it was no longer their interested field of study yet they still needed their job.

A college degree is not a seal of approval that verifies that an individual is fit for a position working and teaching in the early childhood development and education field. It can be a plus or a negative depending on an individual basis. It does not guarantee an employee will be paid more than the caregiver and teacher with years of experience or someone without a college degree.

Here is another example. A handful of college students working at a private center also attended school full–time and worked second jobs. Additionally, the center hired through the government welfare to workfare training program allowing for Federal Tax Credits. They also hired unpaid interns through a community college. These types of employment practices raise issues of hiring qualified individuals. The students, the unpaid interns, and Workfare recipients, who were hired to work in the center had personal depleted energy levels, sleep deprivation, low morale and were living at a poverty level while working in a highly demanding job, some of them without health insurance.

The parents were paying the highest tuition rate on the market, yet they were not privy to these facts about the individuals caring and teaching their children. This form of administration, as to who to employ, was reminiscent of the culture from the dark ages when the poor, mostly women, were employed to provide child care for wealthy women's children in order to barely keep themselves fed.

For some centers no formal experience and no formal education is needed to become employed at a regulated child day care center. The low tuition child day care centers are employing from a different job pool. Experience may mean babysitting for a sibling. Training will follow after a background check and clearance.

Many franchise centers do require a bachelor degree specifically in early childhood development and education. At some of these types of franchise centers the starting pay is fifteen percent above minimum wage.

The work is demanding, dirty and it challenges daily the safety and health of all the staff. A private family child care provider once told me that the burn out rate for the average child care employee is at a maximum of ten years. She had recently retired when we spoke.

Takeoff the Blinders

Here is an example why it is important to know who is providing the child care and teaching your child. At a center each classroom would employ between two to four teachers at one time. Those teachers would be replaced or interchanged with substitute teachers from outside the center or by full–time substitutes, floaters and other room teachers within the center.

I worked a full day of eight hours from 8:30 am to 4:30 pm in a classroom. I rarely met a parent or did they know I worked in the room with their child because the door opened at 8:00 am and closed at 5:00pm. The children knew about me and most would ultimately tell their parents about what we had done for the day.

There were part–time student teachers who the parents never saw or the kitchen help who were used as fillers in the nap rooms. Floaters were also interchanged between classrooms. Parent helpers sometimes assisted for part of the day even though their child may not be enrolled in that specific classroom. In this situation the parent had no formal education, experience or training in early childhood development and education. There were shifting employment changes filling teacher spots weekly and throughout the year. The directors would transfer a full–time or part–time teacher from one room to another half-way through the year. This is also a common practice in schools with school–aged children.

The constant changing of the main caregiver or teacher plays havoc with a child's ability to learn and develop a stable trusting relationship. Maybe the parents did not want to know these facts because they wanted the teachers, directors and center to take over that responsibility of making decisions for them in relation to their children. This became obvious when the parents were unaware that their children may have had up to ten or more people randomly caring and teaching their child in their assigned room during one week.

Having a high volume of teachers and strangers providing child care and teaching children at this young age is extremely unfair and hard on a child. This type of education contradicts Erikson's Psychosocial Development Theory Stage One—the principles of brain development and relationships with other people early in life. Relationships are the major source of development of the emotional and social parts of the brain—this encompasses social trust and mistrust which depends on consistency and sameness of experience provided by a caregiver.

When a director tells a parent that the room ratio is two to four teachers, the parent should ask if those teachers are the same two to four teachers assigned to the child's room on a daily and weekly basis? Will they be the same team teachers for a long period of time in terms of months or a minimum of a year?

Some parents at the center would hire the center's staff to baby–sit after hours at the child's home. The basis for this hiring practice by the parents was that they trusted the center that employed them. Combine the trust factor and the fact that some of the teachers appreciated the extra cash.

More than once a child by chance would encounter a teacher passing by them in the hallway. The child had no other contact with that specific staff member throughout the day. The child ultimately picked up on the teacher's name in passing and would talk incessantly at home about the teacher to the mother. The parent was unaware of the true nature of the relationship. The parent then asked the teacher to baby–sit at their home based on the recommendation from their child who was 2-years-old. Name dropping was a common occurrence among children in the center, it was a child's game. The babysitting rate paid an average of seven dollars an hour per child in the home from the center's parents.

I remember one teacher declining the offer because she had no idea who the child was who had told his mother her name. Add to this fact that she did not want to be a babysitter and was experiencing burn out after two years of working with children in the center. She had already decided to change her college major.

Each state has different regulations and regulations are always changing. Teacher to child ratio guidelines are a major factor in the industry and an aspect stressed in marketing. When a center or school is awarded additional accreditation, you may request and read the guidelines under that specific added program's policies. Remember perfection in the regulated early childhood education and care business does not exist. It is an ideal view that grows into a business form of synergy created between directors, teachers and parents. What anyone can see depends on that person's expectations and capacity.

A State Standard

Return to the Basics

A state government bureau initiated and sponsored a program to teach and incorporate a new state standard for education in child day care centers, early childhood programs and schools. This pilot program was paid for by a state grant and incorporated into a non–profit organization's educational program along with the state university's system for a higher education.

This was an attempt to create a state standard for education across the board for all early childhood centers and schools. For some educators these same principles and methods were already in practice. For many other educators they were not familiar with the new state educational standard. At this present time the new state educational standard in the teaching profession is not being applied by most caregivers and educators, administrators or in educational facilities.

This new state standard for education was very similar to the teaching method I had experienced more than fifty years earlier at an elementary school in a different state. When I had moved two years later to a new state, I experienced an extreme contradiction in teaching methods and a cultural shock as to how children were treated by teachers and principals. An adaptation of the rote method among other archaic techniques was the accepted state standard for education in the second public school district that I was enrolled in.

The reality to re–educate all educators, early childhood teachers and directors in centers and schools was and continues to be a noble effort in an attempt to bring everyone on the same page. This endeavor on implementing a new state standard for education was and is unenforceable and very often goes undetected in the education industry. To compound matters more, there is a question to who is teaching what and how this new state standard for education is being taught to college students and others who are the teachers of the future. Please refer to the chapter, "Regulations and Training" with the subheading, "Watch Your Words: Big Ears Can Hear."

Many parents, educators and directors are incorrigible in their mindset of what and how they teach and care for children. As for the directors overseeing the teachers in the centers and preschools it is implausible to re–educate most of these types of higher held management positions, let alone high volumes of caregivers and teachers already in the system for many years. This would involve behavior modification of teachers who teach teachers and teachers who teach children. This would involve psychological profiling on an individual basis and it would likely reveal behavior modification is not achievable for many teachers.

To contradict what they were taught previously in schools or what they have been practicing for many years, which in many cases includes their personal signature, will never allow for implementation of a new state standard for education to take full effect across the board. Educating children and adults can be a fun and challenging experience when behavioral problems are not a distraction.

Adult re–education is difficult, even more so, than attempting to re–educate a child. The stubborn—I now it all and I have been doing this job for more than ten years, I have two college degrees and no one is going to tell me what to do now—syndrome is infectious in centers and with certified school teachers, directors, principals, deans and professors in the academia hierarchy.

One part of a new state standard for education required child caregivers, teachers and directors, principals and parents to identify each child as an individual with individual needs. This is accomplished by recognizing the three general categories of temperamental types: flexible, fearful and feisty and includes nine indicators or traits.

Too many teachers and adults attempt to force children into being someone that they are not. They also fail to protect children and their individual temperaments and traits. This may occur when children are teased and bullied by other children and sometimes by adults. The old dictum used by teachers and parents telling children that they should be like so and so is actually a form of emotional abuse and violence.

Common sense tells us that while working with children, it is always best to support nature and to avoid the forced attempt to control and dominate what is innate. Teaching is a form of guidance, it is not meant to control and dominate others.

With the high volume of children enrolled into child day care centers and school classrooms, it is inconceivable how educators can meet a state standard for education to identify children individually in order to meet their needs.

Volume control is the number one priority with large groups of children and this ends up working against recognizing and teaching children on an individual basis.

Speak Up and Be Counted

A parent was looking for an alternative child day care other than the private certified nursery school that her child was enrolled at in the suburbs. She had subsequently withdrawn her child from the preschool.

The parent had encountered a cultural shock when she worked as a parent helper one day. The nursery school's policy for a child, who did not want to participate in a group or assigned activity, was he or she would be forced to stand in the corner to face the wall to be shamed in front of the other children. The other parents who volunteered on a rotation basis were confronted by the new parent on this type of teaching. The parents told her that they thought nothing was wrong with the director's and teachers' methods.

This state licensed and accredited private nursery school showed indifference to the state standard for education of Erik Erikson's Psychosocial Development Theory Stage Two. This involves that shame occurs when the child is overtly self-conscious by the use of negative exposure and self-doubt can evolve. The state certified teachers and parents at this nursery school failed to acknowledge emotional development goals for the children. One of the developmental goals was to be able to recognize that children are special and unique by allowing them to make choices.

Here is another example of why a state standard for education was deemed necessary for disciplining children in all state licensed educational facilities. At a low-end child day care center with a high volume of children, volume control and violent behavioral challenges in this environment encompass most of the work day. The director instructed the workers to use, tie-um-up and tie-um-down in a chair for discipline throughout the day. It begins with a buckle chair.

The first time I saw a buckle chair was at a high-end center. In the latter case it was used only during lunch time to protect the child from themselves and from hurting others.

Enter the Endless Saga

A mother telephoned me extremely upset looking for an alternative from a private preschool program where she had enrolled her adopted child who was three-years-old.

The program and philosophy at this center was to train the children diligently with the ABCs and 123s at the earliest age possible to prepare them for kindergarten. The children were also required to complete homework at home with their parents.

The mother's child failed to perform and meet the center's work standards. In this case the mother was called in for a teacher and parent conference. The director and teacher informed the parent that they suspected her daughter had a learning disability because of her low performance in learning her numbers and letters in relation to the other children in her group in the class.

Naturally being a new mother without hesitation she did as the preschool program director told her to do. She took her daughter to be professionally evaluated and to the mother's relief they found nothing wrong with her child. The evaluator suggested the child should be removed immediately from that type of early childhood program environment and the mother agreed.

The teachers' interpretation of the child's abilities on an individual basis was not a part of their curriculum. This violates the state standard for education. How much damage was the child exposed to from the teachers, directors and other children at this preschool program from the pressure for her to perform and failing her at 3–years–old.

At many child day care centers, preschools and nursery schools the common idea of teaching is to imprint the maximum number of facts and skills upon the children at this early age. This method of education works against learning and nature. The excess of too much forced information onto children too young an age results in childhood ending earlier.

Childhood is replaced by school, learning and performing or passing and failing within the group. As a result, when test scores plummet, the entire process is accelerated and the chain of events continues into even earlier schooling. In contrast, while legislators have the greatest voice in the development of educational policy, the newest reform efforts place high stakes on tests.

This academic and government behavior has continually decreased and eliminated funding for the arts in the classroom. Currently with the introduction of teaching children younger and younger in institutional settings for longer and longer hours under the pretext that children become smarter is deceptive.

If something cannot be immediately grasped, children will not understand it because instant information gathering does not understand. Children may repeat the correct answer but they do not understand it.

Too many teachers, directors and school administrators are applying this concept of education. Parents support and want it and have become part of the delusion as to what and how to teach children in relation to how children learn.

Too often child day care centers and schools are indifferent to Erikson's Developmentally Appropriate Practice in early childhood programs. What is appropriate is based on at least three kinds of information of knowledge: what is known about child development and learning, what is known about the strengths, interests and needs of each individual child in the group, and the knowledge of the social and cultural contexts in which children live.

The early childhood education and child care industry is fueled by parents' demands rooted from their own personal interpretations of what they think their children should be learning in child day care centers and schools.

Performance and rewards become instilled in their thinking and behavior at a very young age. Emotional development goals for children are not being acknowledged or met. This trend is multi–generational in the U.S. It is like a cancer that has spread throughout this nation for generations.

Achieve by Intelligence

At a private center the director instructed the staff who worked in the baby rooms not to hold a baby for more than fifteen minutes. Staff workers were also instructed not to hold the same baby more than once and had to alternate the babies.

The director had incorporated her personal philosophy and signature into this state regulated private child day center whose director and teachers were state certified with a minimum of a Bachelor's Degree in Early Childhood Education and Development. The director's philosophy was that she did not want the babies bonding with a specific worker.

The parents who enrolled their children into this private center were informed during the interviewing process of the center's philosophy and practices. The parents agreed with the director and center's policy. The director was indifferent to the principles of brain development and relationships with other people early in life. Relationships are the major source of development of the emotional and social parts of the brain.

The center's policies contradicted Erikson's Psychosocial Development Theory Stage One—this encompasses social trust and mistrust which depends on consistency and sameness of experience provided by a caregiver.

In the psychological culture of non–parenting in the U.S., parents have allowed an industry to take over the once personal human natural role of being a parent. Erikson's Early Emotional Development for children teaches that to permit the infant or child to have confidence in the world around them would equate to hold the infant when crying.

Regulated child day care centers, preschools or other accredited programs for the care and education of young children does not guarantee that a parent is making the right choice. Parents are unqualified to be parents when they are told and agree to non–social developmental principles being practiced by state certified teachers and caregivers in licensed centers and schools that defy all human natural common sense and innate intelligence.

To care for and teach a child does not equate to making that child smart. Smart does not mean giving the right answer, earning a high score or grade point average. Smart means developing intelligence to process thinking, searching for answers, solving problems, making right choices and not repeating the teacher's words with the only goal is to be given a reward.

Too often parents and educators believe to be smart is to perform by learned repetition of facts and skills. Parents and educators reward children when they perform and achieve high scores. The adults involved in these children's lives are themselves rewarded by praise on how smart their child is. Government incentives reward schools and teachers based on scores and awards.

This type of blueprint replicates itself among adults who are rewarded in systems of academics and forms of employment when they repeat the automated correct answers they were told to repeat or what people want to hear. Though they may be incompetent or lack a conscience when graduating from school or while employed in their vocation, they will unfortunately succeed in this form of social structure.

It is not about the Peter Principle, it is about a cultural system that rewards and protects inadequacy performed by adults who are emotionally undeveloped as they go all–out for success by talking their way to the top, forming alliances or by using un–scrupulous methods to obtain social positions and monetary gains.

Intelligence means teaching children to be consciously aware about knowing and realizing how the individual arrived at the answer. It is not about the answer and expecting a reward.

All humans are born with intelligence. How to listen and to find interior intelligence can only be achieved by giving affection, love and acknowledgment to children through acceptance by the parents or caregivers and teachers.

Emotional human development goals need to be met before intelligence can begin to develop. This includes all children on an individual basis and at all ages from the moment of birth.

FOOD

Feed the Children

The Child and Adult Care Food Program (CACFP) is a federally funded program of the Food and Nutrition Service (FNS), United States Department of Agriculture (USDA). The State Department of Health, Division of Nutrition is the administrative agency for the CACFP. The CACFP was established in 1968 as an experimental program to help ensure that children received nutritious well balanced meals while in regulated child cares and schools.

The child day care center must be licensed or registered in order to participate in this program. Child and adult day care centers and schools must serve meals meeting CACFP meal pattern requirements and allow their center or school to be monitored. Centers and schools must maintain menus as records that include meal count records, attendance records and attend training annually and any additional mandatory classes.

Each regulated child day care center and school has its own food policy. A regulated child day care center may or may not be a participant of the CACFP. Don't assume that the food being served by participating centers and schools enrolled in the CACFP program is identical because it is not. During the interview and in the center's contract it should address and outline the specific food policy. If it is not written in their policy, then the parent should ask what it is.

The CACFP dictates five food components for a meal including milk and not less than two components for a snack from specific different food groups, alternating both within a set number of hours. Remember that most policies and regulations will change as new nutritional and behavioral information is gathered by U.S. government studies.

Read the Different Recipes

The numerous accounts I heard from parents in relation to food never had a common ground, unless considering each one's diversity equating to a commonalty. On one occasion two different parents working in the educational field came to interview at my center. One of the parents was a vegetarian and fed their child only vegetarian foods. The other parent fed their child highly processed food. The processed food parent's emphasis for her child was not on what he ate but as long as he ate something.

In the mornings a health-care working professional two parent team, fed their three children donut holes in their car on the way to preschool. A school teacher working towards earning her master degree in an administrative area of education fed her child Hostess snack cakes and milk for breakfast before he was dropped off at the preschool. She stated that was the only food he would eat for breakfast and that her child never ate vegetables so she never made them at home.

At a preschool the teachers were required under CACFP regulations to offer and encourage children to eat all the food components placed on their food trays. The child who never ate vegetables at home did eat vegetables during lunch time at the preschool with no complaints.

These parents are prime examples of how differently we all think about food and we pass that on to our children. Naturally when there is consistency, children eat what is given to them in the home. When parents expect their children to be fed almost exclusively by centers, schools and by others, food then becomes an obscure commodity. Children's relationship with food becomes corrupted in an unnatural manner. These children eat mostly processed food that is cooked by others or bought through food service vendors or prepared behind a cafeteria wall.

Children have become removed from the entire natural process of learning how to plan, shop, prep and cook whole foods. This is a simple daily living skill that ultimately leads to eating. In a natural environment a child learns through the adults these living skills and what types of food is appropriate or acceptable to eat.

In some homes it is a family affair to teach these nutritional skills to children. The children learn what is expected and accepted from them because they are being taught over and over again by the adult family members and are part of the process.

The parent who did not cook or serve her child vegetables at home was teaching her child not to eat vegetables. The child was four–years–old going on five and was overweight, and morbidly obese. The parent had forfeited her role of teaching her child this basic living skill.

It is not a mystery that this country's future generations of children, as they grow into adults, will not have the living skills to shop, prep and cook whole foods. They most likely will not have the living skills to plan a menu.

I heard similar complaints from a parent about her children. The children had repeatedly told the parent that they would never want to or have to cook when they moved away from home because they would buy take–out or prepared food. The parent laughed as she said, "They better have good jobs that pay well if they think they are going to do that."

Uncover the Culpability

With the first onset of their child vomiting the primary source the parents blame is the food served to their children at the centers or schools. I saw and heard this same reaction repeatedly from different parents at different centers. Many of these parents did not practice general good nutrition or make healthy meals for their children at home and this included food safety.

If the entire center or even a cluster of children became sick from the center's food, then I could understand the parent's way of thinking and accusations. This was never the case. In all of the occurrences that I witnessed, it was a single child out of a group who would vomit and the parent would automatically blame food contamination from the center. Maybe the junk food or overeating played a role in their child vomiting.

It must be noted here that the spread of e–coli or other food contagions does exist in rare incidences in centers, schools, homes and restaurants. In the cases I am stating here the source of food contamination or overeating was not from the centers. My advice for parents is, when in doubt check it out immediately with a health-care professional.

In the case of some of the children in my center, food contamination was coming from their home and overeating. The parents would leave cooked food or take–out food on top of the cold stove for twenty four hours or overnight. It was a family practice rooted from multiple generations. This style of eating was established for family members to eat what was available when they wanted it. Meals were never planned. It was a family routine that resulted in a feast or famine home environment and also did not include family sit down style meals. My encouragement to the parents to change this unsafe food practice was met with full resistance.

Take–out food while on the run and feeding children junk food in cars was the accepted practice by every parent who had children enrolled in my center. This same type of behavior was mimicked by the parents at a high–end center.

These sorts of unhealthy food practices also facilitate hand to mouth carrying of viral or bacterial infections with children eating with unclean hands. Additionally, take–out food is handled by many hands behind the counter before it reaches the children's hands, resulting in a higher incident of cross-contamination.

Change the Recipe

My center's first food policy included homemade Mediterranean vegetarian dishes. The nutritional value in these meals exceeded the recommended nutritional value and required components by the CACFP guidelines. In a contradiction these types of Mediterranean meals failed to meet the nutritional guidelines under the CACFP.

They were deemed as unacceptable under the federal food program because the agency interprets style of food when determining whether it is acceptable for children or not. The Mediterranean main entrées were not separated by individual food components on a plate or tray for the children to see as individual food in the meal.

All of the children in my child day care center ate the meals without any difficulty or complaints. The U.S. perpetuates the myth that children will only eat what they can individually pick and choose on a plate otherwise they will not eat it. This is learned behavior passed on by adults.

According to CACFP guidelines the nutritional content could not be effectively measured by each serving in the Mediterranean entrées. There was no guarantee in even distribution of the protein, vegetables and carbohydrates to assure equal nutritional content by individual portions. The vegetables exceeded three times the CACFP requirements. This type of scrutiny made the Mediterranean entrées non–acceptable under the CACFP guidelines.

What would Mediterranean countries say of the CACFP requirement when applied to what and how for generations Mediterranean children and adults have been fed with whole foods cooked into main dishes?

The key factor to learn from some other countries and cultures is that adults and children eat the same meals and together. This is how children for millennium have learned to prep, cook and eat food. It comes from the family and not institutions, food vendors or government agencies. Nor does this fundamental knowledge come from children's nutritional re–education programs. All of which sometimes appear bias when it comes to feeding children healthy and nutritional whole foods in the U.S. Too many parents continue to adopt these culturally preconceived ways of thinking when it comes to children and food, they then pass it on to their children and it becomes multi–generational.

The food policy changed at my center when the number of enrolled children increased. The principles of using fresh produce, avoiding processed foods, use of organic foods when available and incorporating these ingredients remained on the center's menu. The menus alternated seasonally from world vegetarianism to French, Italian, Greek, Latin American, and North American meals.

As part of the center's program and curriculum, children from ages two and older were taught how to help and cook in the kitchen or at the dining room table. All children were required to help clean up after meals. These living skills in the kitchen reinforced basic math, reading and identification skills. The application of science and art were used in the creation of what was made for that day.

The menu changed again as my center's child enrollment once again increased. I alternated between Chinese, Vietnamese and Thai food. These meals were made from scratch, were less time consuming and less expensive to make than the previous menus. The children were exposed to all of the ingredients that they were preparing for their meals.

The children at the center stopped eating their lunches at the public schools and Head Start. Subsequently their parents stopped feeding their children meals at home which they seldom ever did before. Planning, shopping, preparing and cooking meals were not part of the family dynamics. When the children of five arrived at my center they started bulking up.

Under the CACFP guidelines children must be offered second helpings and allowed additional servings when they ask and if it is available. At my child day care center the children were eating me out of business.

Meet Two CACFP Directors

More than fifteen years ago a home cook with a Bachelor's Degree in Nutrition Science was in charge of a local supervising office for the CACFP. She was experienced and passionate in her work. She collected recipes and understood many different techniques and concepts of preparing whole foods. Her knowledge of nutrition and perception of food were beyond what was needed for the job. She continued to fulfill her own passion of learning on the subject matter in her personal time.

Eventually she retired from her position as a director and supervisor for the CACFP. Subsequently the supervising office for the CACFP program introduced a new CACFP director. My child day care center's menus were abruptly no longer reimbursed for meals.

The new CACFP monitors hired by the new director and supervisor could not correctly read the menus. One of many new problems was that the monitors assumed the Asian dishes served at my center came from a bag of frozen processed food. Along with the new CACFP staff a new administrative policy went into practice of not to call CACFP participants when a question or typo occurred on a menu that the monitor didn't understand. The previous management was trained on how to professionally use the telephone when in doubt.

The new management used the slash and burn method of automatically denying reimbursement from the program due to a lack of understanding in basic food preparation with whole foods.

The new supervisor and staff had limited personal experience and knowledge on cooking. They had come from multiple generations that had been raised on fast food and processed food. The new director and the other monitor's educational building blocks were rooted in what they had learned and grown up with during their own childhoods.

Mistakes escalated from the CACFP monitors assigned to my child day care and other centers. During one visit a CACFP monitor arrived at my center when my business was closed for vacation. The CACFP office had been informed in writing on the scheduled dates that my center would be closed.

At some stage of the CACFP monitor's visit I politely mentioned that I was having dinner with my family and that I had previously notified her office that my business was closed. The monitor responded: "I can come here any time I want to." Whether what the CACFP monitor told me was true or not, it was evident that it was an abuse of power by a government contracted non-profit agency food monitor.

This type of thinking and behavior defeats the entire function of the CACFP food monitoring program during child day care centers' scheduled meal times. The previous supervisor would conduct CACFP inspections by coordinating her unannounced visits with scheduled sit down meal times. All regulated child day care centers have mandatory record keeping for weekly menus that clearly outline scheduled meal times on a daily basis.

One day while I prepared a Thai meal for seven children, including two of my own children, I had an unannounced visit for a meal inspection from the new CACFP supervisor. She had not arrived during the scheduled sit down meal time but during the prep time. All of these time intervals are pre–documented, on file and are regulated. The supervisor's office has copies of these records for all centers. In each center it is mandatory for centers to follow the documented scheduled slots of times exactly.

The previous management would arrive unannounced at the scheduled sit down mealtime with the main goal of causing very little disruption with the safety and welfare of the children while performing monitoring duties under the CACFP guidelines. The new supervisor required me to converse with her and answer her questions while I cared for seven children, prepped and cooked the center's dinner with her standing in my kitchen. The supervisor then answered a personal call on her cell phone and started a long conversation in the middle of the evaluation while in my kitchen.

For the readers who need further understanding of the CACFP supervisor's behavior that compromised the welfare and safety of the children, please refer to the chapter heading, "Interviewing" with the subheading, "Don't Panic."

Say Goodbye

More CACFP participants complained about the escalating problems that they were experiencing with the new CACFP management and monitors. The immediate response from the operational director was that a state government agency had given the supervising CACFP office a merit award for excellence. In other words, there was no basis or platform for participants to complain as the merit award was a seal of approval.

My center withdrew participation in the CACFP. Other centers attempted to fight the office's new administration while some centers began to withdraw from the program and attempted to find alternatives. The money being reimbursed by the CACFP to my center could not justify the consistent time consuming disruptions and disputes that my center had been experiencing from the new administrative staff.

My center's food policy changed again. The new food policy became B.Y.O.—bring your own, food, no junk food please. One parent in the center brought organic food. Another parent brought highly processed food. The third parent brought whatever she could scrounge up at the last minute. Under state regulation the center is responsible to fill in the nutritional gaps by supplementing the food if and when there were any from the parents.

A previously established aspect of the center's food policy included that all food that the children brought in their hands or mouths during drop–off would be immediately confiscated. The junk food and milk or other fluids would either be thrown out or saved to take home later. Usually most everything was thrown out because the food and drinks looked like they had been around the block a few times.

For more than a decade the widespread problem with the junk food in the child's hand or mouth at drop–off never ceased. I saw the same problem at a high–end center. These parents use junk food as a reward system in the transitioning process to child day care centers or schools. This reinforces emotional food eating and addiction by using food as a reward.

In many of these cases the child had no previous problems in the transitioning process from home to center. It was the parents who were creating the problem for their children and for the teachers who were put into the role of removing the junk food from the children's possession.

It was also a common practice for some centers' parents not to feed their children meals at home. Lack of money was usually not the main cause for this parental behavior. Some parents for multiple generations had been raised on CACFP meals as soon as they entered Head Start and continued with the entitlement program up through high school and summer food programs.

The CACFP's good intentions have created a backlash. Parents mistakenly believe that it is the role of the government, centers and schools to feed their children. These multi–generational families were never taught or learned to plan, shop, and prep, serve or clean up meals for their children. They did learn that government educational services do the work for them and it is usually free.

The children of one family that was enrolled in my center placed their children also in Head Start and public school. The children arrived at the center in the afternoons and stayed through the evenings. The Head Start children were being fed two meals and one snack. Later on in the day they were fed one meal and two snacks at my center. The same meal patterns were provided to the older children who would transfer from school into the center.

When the children were on summer break from school they ate nothing before coming to the center. I was providing two meals and one snack under the CACFP. On occasion the father or grandmother would randomly take the children out for fast food on a reward system, right before drop–off or immediately following child day care pick–up.

This is not isolated only to my center but also an occurrence at private centers. The strong message that is sent by these parents is that they do not have to take responsibility to feed their children meals because centers and schools will do it for them. Some parents do not want to eat with their children for various reasons. There are too many parents who misunderstand the role a parent has to feed their children.

Credit needs to be given to the experienced and passionate first CACFP director. She and the monitors under her direction conducted themselves in a professional manner. She supported centers in her dedicated and hard work while giving solid good advice on how to deal with sensitive common food issues relating to children and their challenging parents.

Her words of advice: "once that child enters through your door, you are in charge; they are in your child day care and under your child day care policies".

Think Responsibly

At a state annual educator's conference, a child day care proprietor from another part of the state informed me that she had dropped the CACFP from her group center. In support of her center's food policy the parents united together and made arrangements to collect and donate organic vegetarian food to the child day care center. The CACFP's mandatory milk component for all children became one of many issues that her group center and parents did not agree on. The battle lines were drawn and the wars began until finally her group center had dropped the CACFP.

At a child day care center on a state university campus, the center's food policy was to have the child bring a bagged lunch, snacks and no junk food. One parent decided the center's no junk food policy violated his child's rights. The parent filed a lawsuit against the child day care center.

At a private center they provided processed fatty meals for breakfast and lunch. The menu was reminiscent of traditional American food from the mid–twentieth century. Most of the teachers would not eat the food. Most of the children liked the high–carbohydrate processed starches and fatty processed meats. Most of the vegetables and the fruit were also processed.

These examples show how food menus are influenced by the proprietor or director's personal signature, yet all of these centers follow the mandatory guidelines listed under the CACFP–USDA federal program.

At a private center the parents were assigned individually to contribute food designated for the afternoon snacks. The CACFP did not reimburse this allocated snack because there is a cap for the number of scheduled meals and snacks reimbursed within a certain time frame per day. This regulation applies to all enrolled centers and schools. The parents were responsible at one week intervals to donate snacks for individual classrooms of children.

In the room for children that were four-years-old, parents donated snacks that were eventually thrown into the trash can ninety–percent of the time by all of the children. The food was highly processed and bought in bulk by the individual parents with the main thought behind it being the cost. This type of food was untouched due to lack of better judgment on the part of the parents and the teachers who organized the snack list for weekly donations.

Food represents who we are and who we will become over the course of time. Chemical and emotional food addictions are multi–generational and endemic in the U.S. This brings back the original question, who is teaching and raising the children?

THE LAW

Find the Thin Blue Line

Having a parent and child come into any child day care center or school on a consistent daily routine opens up all sorts of questionable behavior on parenting issues that caregivers and teachers will see and know about but others will not. It becomes a professional role that is sometimes subjective for the caregivers and teachers on when and how to broach a problem occurring in the child's home environment.

It is not strange or paradoxical that each parent sees regulated child day care providers, educators and teachers in different ways. What anyone can see depends on that person's expectation and capacity. Some people cannot recognize that all regulated child day care centers and schools are mandatory reporters for the government. A report is made when licensed or registered child day care employees, educators or teachers have reasonable cause to suspect that a child coming before them is an abused or maltreated child.

Knowing and proving what the center or teacher knows to a third party is not always realistic. There is another type of problem with some parents who have at–risk children enrolled in a child day care center. Some parents are diagnosed with serious mental disorders, have less than a fifth grade education, have criminal records with violent backgrounds, or are war refugees from underdeveloped countries and some are none of these but have at–risk children.

In many of these challenging situations the parents in my center had a team of second, third and fourth party government agency workers assigned to their cases. The assortment of agencies had a central job to diligently protect the best interests of the parents. This included protecting the parental rights of these parents to keep full custody of their children.

The protection of the children was not part of their administrative government agency's field but another administrative department's jurisdiction. It created a conflict of interest in more than one case I experienced. On one occasion two social workers assigned to protect the parent's rights became overzealous with their priorities. In this case my position as a mandatory state reporter conflicted with their position, yet I was coordinating my professional position to work with all parties involved. I was falling back on my private corporate management training and was not familiar at the time with the intrinsic ways of government agencies and civil servants. In retrospect it is like comparing apples to oranges.

For example: a parent had been diagnosed at age fifteen with paranoid schizophrenia and bipolar manic depression. She had a fifth grade level of education, was dangerous to herself and others and had five children from unfamiliar and various men. Four of the children had been removed from her guardianship. The court had granted the mother supervised visitation with those children. Each time a child was removed from her care she would become pregnant again. She was often homeless and when she became pregnant with her fifth child and with the added fact of her prior diagnosis for a serious mental disorder already on record, the government expedited her case to the top of the five–year waiting list for subsidized government housing.

Due to her violent criminal record and other behavioral problems, any form of consistency in her home life was not realistic even with the support of teams of government agencies. It was undeniably in the best interest of the fifth child to be permanently removed from her care. This statement is not made lightly.

The shock from this case was due to the fact that the social workers assigned to the parent's care did everything possible to protect the parent's rights to keep the child and not the child's rights. A vicious circle was co–created in a co–dependent working relationship. During my involvement with this case the child remained with the mother after the child was terminated from enrollment in my center. The infant was then placed in a low–end child care center facility. By the age of nine months the child had been in and out of five government subsidized contracted regulated child day care centers while the mother was seeking court ordered medical treatment and attending court hearings.

Discover the Gray Area

In most circumstances a reputable and good regulated child day care center will make recommendations and try to work with the parents when there is a suspected problem. No child day care center can force a parent to change their behavior around their child in their home. In some instances, centers have taken over the responsibility of remedying the neglect of children because circumstances dictated it as an alternative of calling in a third party. This is by no means enabling the parent. It usually involves protecting a child's health opposed to the child and family being thrown into a bureaucratic boondoggle when time is of the essence and the remedy is straightforward.

Calling in a third party may cause the parent to feel betrayed and the outcome will be that nothing becomes accomplished. Experience has shown many teachers and centers that while working with at–risk children, bringing a third party into the parent's life is most likely not going to rectify the problems. Other centers have also been placed in this position, sometimes involving child health-care issues that the parents could not navigate through.

In one case I had no alternative left but to make the report to the State Central Register (SCR). The parent had been diagnosed with bipolar manic depression and had a history of violence. The mother of the child had surrendered full custody to the mentally ill father when the child was very young. In this particular case the parent's state caseworker gave me their full support. As time progressed it was clear that it was time to call in SCR. After Child Protective Services (CPS) conducted a second home visit, the father immediately sold his car and fled the state with his child of 3-years-old.

Some parents who had children enrolled into my center had been prescribed medication for serious mental disorders. These parents collected social security under the disabilities act. Weekly professional psychiatric counseling or monitoring by a mental health-care worker was not mandatory in one of these cases. It may be conditional on an individual case basis but it was not mandatory.

More than one social case worker for these at-risk parents suggested that I should have the parents be in attendance at my center while their children were present to better help with the parent's separation anxiety. This sort of unprofessional and irresponsible recommendation from county and state government social workers is unconscionable.

That type of proposal raises all sorts of questions on the safety and welfare of all the children in the center's care and creates an extremely high liability for the business. These parents were in need of adult day care and consistent monitoring of their medication use with weekly or daily counseling. Random home visits were useless in two of these cases. The parents had medical and criminal records with a history of very violent behavior. A regulated child care center is not in the business as an adult day care center for at–risk parents while in the company of numerous young children in the same room.

The distraction alone from any one of the three very emotionally needy parents would make it impossible to operate a regulated child day care center's program under state regulations. These parents were socially violent, school drop–outs, were abandoned by their families and had severe daily social behavioral challenges.

Their emotional pendulum swung from presenting the perfect socially adapt caring human persona to extreme maliciousness, apathy, with imagined threats of persecution dominated by perverse acts of revenge that they (the parents) carried out. Self–destruction by these parents was always imminent. To see the infants and young children in the cross fire when it occurred was an educational shock.

The parents stopped using their meds during certain time-lines or used alcohol to self-medicate in addition to their meds. This was not the foundation of their violent behavior when they became dangerous to themselves and everyone connected to them. The procreation of the children resulted from two adults who had no emotionally, intimate or physically established attachments. The conceptions took place with anonymous strangers despite the fact of being homeless or in the government's independent living programs.

In all of these cases the other biological parent surrendered all legal rights of the child to the diagnosed mentally ill parent and thereafter disappeared after being battered through the courts by a line of attack from the diagnosed mentally ill parent, supported by their government case workers. Numerous government agencies and the courts became the single parent's new type of surrogate family system. To raise a child is a full–time job twenty–four hours a day seven days a week for a life time. Judges and other government employees work Monday through Friday excluding holidays and vacations, their work day ends at 5 pm.

The mandatory reporter law places regulated centers and school teachers in a professional hot seat while they try to maintain a delicate balance between a government bureaucratic system with parents and their at–risk children. Consequently, the best interest of the child becomes secondary or lost altogether.

The developmental emotional needs of these children in these three cases will never be met. This one fact alone out of many perpetuates the family cycle of violent behavior when the home is filled with chaos and unpredictability. That child becomes part of an unnatural order.

These children mentioned above will never meet Maslow's Hierarchy of Needs. The first of which is the basic physiological needs of hunger, thirst, sleep, shelter. The second is safety, to feel secure, safe and out of danger. The third is belongingness and love, to affiliate with others, be accepted and belong. The fourth is esteem, to achieve, be competent, and gain approval and recognition. The fifth is cognitive needs, to know, understand and explore. The sixth is aesthetic needs, symmetry, order and beauty.

The seventh is self–actualization needs to find self-fulfillment and realize one's potential. In these three cases, the first need and let alone the other needs, of all of the children was not met in the home.

In order to channel Maslows Hierarchy of Needs the first need has to be met before making the lead to the next one or alternating others. The at–risk children on Mondays would be dropped off at my center. It would take one to two days to rework the children's highly intense state of their physiological and psychological condition that they had arrived in.

The children would begin to mend and become well, cheerful and productive throughout the week up until pick–up on Fridays. The following Monday the cycle would start over again with the highly demanding and sensitive remedial work with these children. What happened on the weekends when the children went home would ultimately reverse all of the hard work that was accomplished during the week.

As a state mandatory reporter, whether to make a report to SCR when in almost all cases CPS can do nothing, unless there is physical evidence and much documentation, is a difficult position to be placed in.

Create a Flawless Law

In one case at an educational workshop an assistant director discussed her experience about a parent who owed her center money. The parent had removed her child from the center and left an unpaid debt. She then placed her child in another center. The mother continued this pattern of behavior with one child day care center after another.

The director of one of the victimized centers pursued the parent to collect the outstanding debt. When the center's director attempted to collect the debt, the parent then retaliated by reporting the center to CPS. This form of retaliation against centers and schools, for numerous reasons, takes place every day in the U.S.

This type of retaliation is costly. Intentional filing of false reports creates high liability with insurance and expensive attorney's fees. This malicious behavior distracts from the main purpose of regulated centers and schools, which is the focus of care and education of children.

At a state annual educational conference, a workshop was held for all educators and teachers on the ongoing problem of false allegations, due to the fact that it occurs on a consistent basis.

There is a state social service law for filing false reports when used as a means of retaliation. In order to enforce this law, it has to be proven beyond a doubt that the individual intentionally filed the false report. The initial stage would require the victim of a false report to pay for and hire a lawyer for legal proceedings. After battling the false allegations through the government administrative agency's investigation and legal proceedings in court, then the process for filing an intentional false report would be made. If successful, the parent/ person who filed the false allegations would be fined ten thousand dollars. In the case previously mentioned the basis for filing the false allegations in the first place, was refusal to pay for services rendered.

Children's parents and their extended family members who falsely accuse caregivers and teachers in centers and schools, is an ongoing social problem in the U.S., which no one likes to openly discuss in the industry. It is an endless business and professional nightmare that will never stop in the child care and education industry.

The simple undertaking of making a phone call to CPS while initiating the act of retaliation gives the offending adult instant gratification and the power over the victim. The two main objectives from the perpetrating adult are—to instill fear dominated by the perverse act of revenge and secondly to gain control over the victim. This is the true intent behind retaliation, it is learned behavior.

Under law every report to CPS has to be investigated no matter how frivolous the complaint may be. Actual child abuse is a very serious offense. False allegations of child abuse are also a very serious offense. Both goals by the perpetrators of these acts of violence are to victimize the most innocent.

Be Aware

All licensed educators and schools, including all regulated child day care centers are state mandatory reporters. Certain professionals are required by law to report suspected child abuse or maltreatment to a State Central Register (SCR). The law also assigns civil and criminal liability to those professionals who do not comply with their mandated reporter responsibilities.

The collaboration relationship between regulated child day care centers, schools and the child protective services as mandatory reporters is one example of a government link.

Other government agencies have established an association with both regulated child day care centers and schools. Police agencies may release certain information to regulated child day care centers and schools about registered sex offenders under the provisions of the state Sex Offender Registration Act also known as Megan's Law.

My regulated child day care center received notification from the police of Level 3 and other levels of sex offenders living in the area. Level 3 means that there is a high–risk of re–offending and a threat to public safety. More than seven public schools were located in a one and a half mile radius of my center.

Each state may apply laws differently based on jurisdiction or by the calendar year. The reader is responsible to check out the laws in their own state. Understand that government laws and policies change continually.

A LICENSOR

Follow the Regulatory Trail

The title has changed over the years from Day Care Inspector, Licensor, Case Worker or Child Day Care Registrar. These individuals are civil servants working through a county or in some jurisdictions a city agency hired through a state government agency.

The licensors are responsible for the issuance, renewing and denying of a regulated child day care center's license or registration. A licensor is responsible for the field work of inspection of a child day care center. They handle all of the administrative work of submitting the applications or renewals into the government's data base. The licensor is in charge of data base cross referencing with other government agencies such as CPS. They also update information while at the same time making sure the child day care centers are keeping in compliance with state regulation changes.

In one case a social worker changed their occupation from a CPS investigator to a regulated child day care licensor. This individual had worked in the CPS unit for many years and was familiar with the neighborhood in which I had opened my child day care center. During our first meeting the licensor wanted to become acquainted. He had asked why I would want to start a regulated child day care center in the neighborhood that I was located in?

At that time, I did not know that enrollment for child day care centers are more often than not based upon local neighborhood population. My thinking back then was what could go wrong with my good intentions and hard work. In retrospect the licensor was forewarning me about the repercussions of working with families in a transient urban environment with the majority of at–risk children that were highly government subsidized.

Please Take Off Your Shoes

Years later my child day care center's administrative regulatory duties were assigned to a new licensor. One day a little bit before two o'clock a United Parcel Service truck made a delivery to the center. The two infants enrolled at the time were taking their scheduled naps. The school–aged children were scheduled to arrive later that afternoon.

I opened the delivered box and inside was a Kitchen Aid 6 Qt.525 Watt Professional Stand Mixer. The children in my center had made numerous breads including pizza dough by hand. They could now make bread, cookies and just about everything with the new stand mixer.

Soon after the delivery there was another knock at the door and standing there were two licensors to conduct an unannounced inspection of the center. A senior licensor was present as an observer only and the other licensor was in charge of the inspection.

As a courtesy to the local government's child day care unit I had previously submitted my business operating hours for my center and the schedule of when I home schooled. It was clear that there was no conflict of interests with the home schooling and the center's hours of operation. That was the only information that they needed to know in practical terms of business operations. Otherwise that government administrative agency placed the state in violation of a federal law under the Family Educational Rights and Privacy Act (FERPA).

I thought the legal conflict of government jurisdictions in reference to my center had been brought to a close. On that autumn afternoon it came to a full circle. It was the only thought the newly assigned licensor had on her mind. My younger son sat at the dining room table as he flipped through his older brother's math book. My older son was working at the computer when the two licensors came into the center. I had started to lift parts of the stand mixer out of the box. I then began to put the stand mixer parts back into the box when the licensors entered into my dining room.

The licensors walked through the center with caked mud and leaves on the bottom of their shoes. The new licensor proceeded to raise her voice in front of my children and demanded: "what's this book doing on the table... what are these books for, it looks like you are home schooling to me, you better not be home schooling, the county doesn't pay you to home school, are you home schooling?" My reply: "no, my children are doing independent study. I was opening up a box for a stand mixer." The licensor loudly snapped back; "Oh, so you are home schooling?"

My sons freely and independently would read, write and study. This is behavior that comes naturally with most home schooled children, curiosity and sharing of books, and the computer. Books could be found on almost every surface, drawer and cabinet. The linen built–in wall cabinet was stacked with rows of books. The kitchen cabinet had three shelves with rows of books. The child day care reading center had six shelves of children's books.

There was a local TV news segment that showed home schooling through one point of view. The family sat down at the kitchen table for six consecutive hours with store bought curriculum and text books. I did not home school with that type of method, nor would ever use such an approach to teach a child or adult in that manner.

Education styles for home schooling differ greatly from one another and are infinite in possibilities when applied on an individual basis. The technique that I applied was John Holt's— Cambridge, MA—method of teaching.

On that particular day it was affirmation why licensors and their government administrative agency do not have the legal jurisdiction to cross over into another government department's jurisdiction of expertise and authority. The new state child day care center regulation is a conflict of jurisdictions of government agencies. It would take a hired legal team to overturn this state regulation that violates federal law.

FERPA was passed into law in order to protect students and their family's privacy from other government agencies. Licensors are not educators and the government's hiring practices do not require a formal education or experience in early childhood education, childhood and human development or any background in education to qualify for the position. They do not require a college degree in lieu of some sort of experience. Licensors are not required educators from any echelon of the government or private sectors.

Licensors do not have the professional experience or training in the selective and highly diverse field of home schooling. That jurisdiction of education belongs to a separate entity of the government: The Home Schooling Office at the Department of the Board of Education.

The new state regulation gave the licensors the illegitimate authority (abuse of power) of disclosure of all school records for all home schooling students filed with and approved by the Department of the Board of Education.

Licensors are trained by a government agency to perform an administrative task. A licensor is an on–site inspector for regulated child day care centers.

This particular licensor violated the state standard for education of Erik Erikson's Psychosocial Development Theory for the emotional development of children in regulated child day care centers and early childhood programs in schools. Both of the licensors had compromised the safety and welfare of all of the children in my care. This included the two babies who had been asleep.

The licensor's violent behavior, apathy and desire to instill fear with threats to dominate by acts of revenge were rooted in her childhood developmental, education and likely embedded in her family and extended social environment. Her emotional developmental needs had not been met during her early childhood education and care. The licensor's form of violent behavior around children and adults was learned behavior. Additionally, she was taught in life that it was acceptable by her peers, and that included civil servants.

In my center all shoes were removed at the door for the safety of the children and especially with the crawling babies. The licensor's failure to use an inside voice, awoke one baby in the middle of his scheduled nap. That baby then woke up the other baby as the licensor continued with her violent behavior. Her act of shaming my two children and their mother raises all sorts of questions in relation to all of the children's sense of security and safety being violated.

This licensor did not have the training or background in education, human behaviorism and development, psychosocial development of children and this included the teaching method of independent study. Refer to the chapter, "A Profession" with the subheading, "Meet My Educators."

The senior licensor stood quietly by as she watched this scene unfold. When the licensor's violent behavior with the sole aim to instill fear in me continued to escalate, the observer quietly explained to the licensor what independent study entailed and meant. She then suggested that she move on with the center's inspection. After the licensor could gather no evidence against home schooling while the center was operating, she proceeded to go through every file, paper and room in the center looking for a state regulatory violation.

Don't Cross the Line

All of the documents were quickly produced that the licensor requested. In the conclusion of the visit she got what she wanted. She then left as quickly as she had arrived. When there were no violations to be found, she created one with the intent to harm and to instill fear. The new real horror began with her government unit's threat of terminating my center's registration. The closing of my center would in turn have an effect on many people. First there would be the loss of my immediate livelihood. My child day care comprised of children who had been enrolled in my center for up to four years. These at-risk children would lose the only consistency and stability in their lives.

The asserted violation consisted of a dated signature on a form in one of the parent's files from a doctor. On one out of five of the children's medical files the required date of the new signature was one month overdue on one form. The pertinent information, at my request to the parent, had been recently completed and brought up to date on the form. This medical information was in compliance with state regulations. The licensor filed an official violation of regulations against my center based on that fact resulting with imminent loss of the center's operating registration and immediate cancellation of the center's business contract with the county.

When I attended educational workshops, other experiences were shared of intimidation from licensors. The stories came from educators working in licensed centers, and group and family child day care centers. Some believe part of the abuse of power is because licensors are encouraged to write up as many violations as possible on regulated centers to validate their local government agency's work to the state that contracted the work out to the county. It has been said it is similar in behavior to police upping the ante during certain times of the month by issuing a high volume of tickets to licensed drivers. In both case scenarios they are rewarded by various government-employer remunerations.

In this case the inspector specifically targeted my business because I had spoken up. For more on this subject matter refer to Part 2 under the chapter, "FERPA" with the subheading, "Outline the Collision Course."

What I do know from my first hand experiences in the early childhood education and child care industry, it is random whether a regulated center will be assigned a government licensor that will work with that center or against it.

Part 2

DIFFERENT APPROACHES TO EDUCATION

My FDC

Take a Peek Inside

The decision to open a registered family day care (FDC) center in an inner–city neighborhood was an idealistic intention. I created a curriculum based on natural science, cooperative games and nurturing one–on–one. The core of the curriculum included a strong emphasize on incorporating living skills while teaching the fundamental basic three Rs through play.

The center's program included a strong emphasize on art, children's literature and math. These were incorporated and taught in the courses of gourmet cooking, children's yoga, organic gardening, clay sculpting, drawing, painting, playing and etcetera. The curriculum was a back–to–basic concept of working with small groups of children of different ages, and one–on–one teaching. Reading, writing and arithmetic were introduced in a child friendly way through creative play at a very early age. Teaching art rather than doing crafts emphasized the process rather than the product. The center's program included a morning or afternoon till evening schedule depending on the day of the week based on the parent's FDC contract.

- yoga
- outdoor play
- morning snack
- art and/or baking project
- free play
- lunch time
- brush teeth
- group game
- reading
- nap time
- afternoon snack

- TV time with child friendly nature based shows
- Play group games, calendars, reading, free play
- pickup time

During the center's summer program all of the children of all ages began the day with yoga, followed by working on the porch garden. Then we went to the park or playground when the weather permitted. As a group we moved onto an art or a baking project, sometimes the children did both in the same day.

The children would assist with making lunch or dinner, after eating they were responsible to remove their dishes from the table and then brush their teeth. We then played a non–competitive or mathematically conceptually based group game followed by reading children's literature.

Rest time was scheduled for two hours; this is a state regulation for all early childhood programs, centers and preschools. After the children had taken their naps, they marked and named that day's date on calendars they had individually designed and made for each month. Afternoon snack often consisted of organic vegetables or fruits with a protein or a gourmet baked item the children had made earlier in the day.

The core of my center's Mission Statement encompassed an overwhelming commitment to nurturing and supporting conduct that was nonviolent, non–sexist, non–racist and respectful to others and nature. Integrity, self respect, imagination and discovery were a few of the written philosophies in my center's Mission Statement. The individual program addressed a balance of child and provider directed activities and hands–on learning.

Additionally, the objectives were flexibility of scheduling, few transitions and a consistent adult providing the care and teaching of all of the children. The center integrated teaching multi–sensory learning, ego development, functional social and life skills rather than academics. Learning academics came freely without it being the all–purpose center of attention.

Primarily my method of teaching focused on providing a consistently stable safe and healthy environment while the children's individual needs were met. Daily reliability in my program was a key factor to make this formula work. The center's form of teaching and child care cannot be applied to a center with a high turnover of caregivers and teachers.

This concept cannot work in large volume centers or centers with a high turnover of enrolled children. Discipline was usually not a problem because of the consistency in personal bonding. The reliable daily routine contributed to the children knowing as to what was acceptable and non–acceptable behavior in the center. All of the children's needs were being met.

One example in the program included the children to make birthday cakes as a group when it was one of the other children's birthday and for special occasions. The cakes were made from scratch by using basic ingredients that required reading and measuring by the children. This entailed reading measuring utensils, and words listed on ingredients and in recipes. Over the span of years, the children made almost every cake imaginable and that included making vegan cakes.

Try to Combine Oil and Water

Most but not all of the children in the center were county and state government contracted cases through various government agencies such as preventive services, workfare, eligible low–income, child protective services and through a state program for people who had disabilities. Very few children were under private contract in the center.

Families consisted of single parent households and two parents or extended family members who were responsible for random care of the children. The head of these households changed in many of these cases. Some family's size changed with unplanned pregnancies or with the adult male figure in the household shifting.

I worked in my child day care center nonstop for more than ten years. The income from different government subsidized child care programs barely paid the overhead costs. The rates paid on average were sixty–five percent below the private market. My family lived below the poverty line during this time period.

No child was enrolled for more than nine hours at one time under the full time rate. Some of the children's enrollment schedules were not identical but lapped over each other. This sometimes created a need to work twelve hour days at different intervals with children. In these cases, they were often short term because the parents were transient.

My work— educational, physiological and behavioral—would become negated when the children left my child day care center to return to their numerous caregivers for more than two days at any time.

Government subsidized monthly child day care payments were consistently issued late or invoices or check payments were lost. The government agencies blamed the parents for not returning the completed forms on time. The parents blamed the government agencies for losing the mailed in forms. Both sides were telling the truth and sometimes neither was, depending on which case was involved and at which time it occurred.

Visit the Brick Wall

On average thirty–percent of the parents with children enrolled in the center, were ordered by family court to attend mandatory parenting classes. The classes the parents were trained in had zero effect on the individual's parenting skills or the government's attempts to have the parents learn to take responsibility and change their behavior with their children. Under the management of multiple government case workers, the parenting classes were attended by the parents only as a means to an end, used by the parents to keep legal guardianship of their children.

Any attempt at re–educating an adult from any social, educational or economic background is very challenging. The adult will repeat the right answers the teacher wants to hear but the adult will continue to act out their beliefs and learned behavior from their previous learning experiences. In these parental cases it involved re–educating and not educating.

There was a common thread that bound the parent's point of view on their non–parenting of their unplanned pregnancies. The parents came from all different races, ethnic, cultural and educational backgrounds. Surprisingly most of these parents parented identically and rarely or never spent one–on–one time with their children.

In most of these cases the children's basic needs were rarely met by the parents. There was no consistency with meals and family style meals were nonexistent in the homes. Younger age children were placed in front of a TV with a bottle or food in their possession, this was given by the parents or extended family members while in their care. Food became the parent. TV was their teacher. TV was the mother and the father. Cable TV and rented Hollywood movies was their truth to all life. Fast food and junk food were the reward system and surrogate for love. Food was the tool to keep the children quiet and occupied in front of the TV. The food given to the children always came enclosed in bright colors, shiny wrappers and disposable bags and boxes.

Sleep schedules did not exist in the multitudes of the extended family homes that the children stayed in. Under state regulation the children were required to take a two hour nap in the program at my center and for most all of the parents this was an endless contentious issue between the parents and me. They insisted that if their young infants of children took a nap in the daytime this would prevent their children to sleep during the nighttime.

As a result, the parents allowed their toddlers and older children to watch TV or DVDs until 2am in the morning until they fell asleep in front of the TV. All of these children—private and government contracted—had no consistent sleep schedules and young children's naps were non–existent in their homes.

In harsh contradiction, while in the parent's care the young infants and children would constantly and randomly fall asleep sitting upright in a chair, at a table or on a couch watching TV. This type of home life created an endless cycle of chaos on the physiological systems of the children's young bodies.

Learned behavioral problems were reinforced and established with the parent's unfathomable beliefs about young children and sleep, while sleep was viewed as a reward or punishment and not as a human physiological need.

The effect and importance of sleep in child and adult human development mirrors each other in its effect on the chemical processes in the brain as well as behavior and learning. It is like day and night—sleep deprivation versus well rested- in human behavior outcome.

This type of environment in the children's home life created a shell of an existence. The extended large number of family members, including grandmothers and fathers, aunts, step–mothers, boyfriends and step–fathers, were not included on the third party government contract with my center. Yet their overwhelming presence, intentional interference, sabotage, derogatory language directed at me in front of all the children under my care and their incessant arguing about the enrolled children's daily program was never–ending.

The multitudes of adults that connected themselves to the children in my center could not move forward from their own lack of education or confrontational behavior. This cycle repeated itself from one generation to the next in the home.

Most of the parents with enrolled children in my center shared one more strong common belief. That during the first three years of life the child's brain was very small and undeveloped. The parents believed that children could not respond to learning, thought, behavior, or memory.

In summary—the parents believed that children ages from newborn to around three–years–old, that their intelligence and aptitude were very limited due to the brain size. This belief system was so strong in this erroneous belief that the parents held their children not responsible for their behavior under the age of three. The parents believed that their children did not have the mental capacity to start learning until around the age of three. It was this type of thinking that allowed the parents to have little or no interaction or communication with their infants and young children.

Additionally, most all of the parents believed that genetics were the key factor in how smart their child would become combined with placing their children early into school. I experienced this cultural shock repeatedly from mothers and fathers that were fourth and fifth generation Americans, newly migrated parents from underdeveloped countries and the seriously mentally ill parents.

The fallacy of infants and young children having no innate intelligence was passed on from mothers to mothers while supported and practiced by the fathers from one generation to the next generation of parents. Trying to teach, explain or inform the parents of the true facts was comparable to talking to a rock in a glacial abyss.

Archaeological archives have documented that during Roman times infanticides were a common and socially accepted practice as long as the child was under the age of two. During this period of time children ages two and younger were not buried in cemeteries, it is believed because the children were not considered to be whole humans—infants and young children had neither souls nor intelligence.

My modern hypothesis with the present day non–parenting practices and thinking comes from the parents' misunderstanding on why the Head Start Program and other government early education programs were initiated by the U.S. government and other world agencies. They were started in order to have the children catch–up and be primed for kindergarten because they were developmentally behind due to the non-parenting from age newborn to three-years -old.

The types of government programs such as Head Start do not accept children under age three for two main reasons. One is the escalating cost factors of such programs. Additionally, the government's early childhood programs wait until age three and older because they were not intended or designed for teaching and caring for younger age children.

The child has to be toilet trained before enrollment is accepted in most any public or private preschool program in the U.S. with the exception of child day care centers, which under regulations require an early childhood program.

More than one parent had enrolled their child into Head Start and my center. Though the children wore pull–ups at Head Start, most every day the children had pee accidents, they were not fully toilet trained. Head Start in my neighborhood was dealing with developmental and behavioral issues including toilet training challenges on a daily basis.

If the same circumstances presented themselves at a private nursery school, the child would most likely not have been accepted for enrollment, and or immediately terminated due to not being ready. At the Head Start program, it was there that many parents from my center had been enrolled when they were between the ages of three and five. In one case a father, as many other parents had done, insisted that Head Start was giving his children an education and that my center was not. This parent became a father of six children and had dropped out of public school in the seventh grade.

What I have learned in the child care and educational industry is that parents incorporate their own interpretations and judgments when it involves child care and educating their children no matter how self–defeating they may be.

Connect and Grow the Pathways

The true facts are that the child's brain is hard at work connecting brain cells. Each time babies and children use their senses through different kinds of experiences it makes connections in the brain stronger. These connections shape the way a child thinks, feels, behaves and learns. Early adult and infant interactions do not just create a context; they directly affect the way the brain is wired. By the time the child reaches the age of three, their brains are twice as active as an adult brain.

Learning starts at birth and education needs to start at birth as well. The first six years of life are critical. To educate children and adults can be fun and very challenging. To re–educate children is a challenge and will be met with resistance, however success is possible. To re–educate an adult usually meets with a higher resistance and becomes highly improbable.

The parents with children in my center believed the fallacy that young children had no ability to learn and had limited intelligence under the age of three. Therefore, their children could not be held accountable for their behavior. Inaction in parenting became the accepted role and the parents in turn ignored their young children. They did not set limits or expectations on their children in relation to behavior or learning during this crucial early age of child development.

Not even a low level of communication was used between most of the parents with their children under the age of three. The parent's behavior supported the false belief that the child could not intellectually comprehend the parent and the accepted practice was physical discipline or no discipline at all.

In some instances, when the situation escalated with the parent, male figure or grandmother's displeasure and frustration, they would use physical discipline daily from a very early age—infant and older—to communicate with the child. It begins as an infant with a slap and graduates to using a belt. Fear would be instilled upon the child early on by numerous family members as a means of power to control the children. Void of nurturing and love makes the outcome for this type of parenting very difficult for professional educators to deal with on a daily basis in centers and schools.

In all of the cases when the children turned three–years–old all the rules of parenting changed and with it what became the socially accepted norm.

At an extended family or social gathering the parents began placement of the three–year–olds in unsupervised groups with older children.

I was repeatedly told this from different parents in my center and that the reason for their parenting choice was because at age three the child was no longer a baby. The children would be split into groups by age and gender at large and small social gatherings. They were encouraged or required to play with the older groups of children. The adults would conjugate into groups. The children had no adult supervision or play interaction.

I remember one boy who was age three being told he was no longer a baby and was then allowed to be included with the adult men's social group. At other times he was placed in large unsupervised groups of the older children. This occurred also with other three–year–old children from families in my center.

In one case a child who was age three returned to my center with more than thirty mosquito bites and sunburn on his body. On the weekends the child had been sent by his father, while in his care, to the other side of the outdoor camp ground to spend the day with no or sporadic limited adult supervision. The child was on his own or in the older children's social group. The parent saw nothing wrong with his parenting choice. This particular father at age five grew up with no mother and his father was emotionally and physically unavailable to him as a child.

The reality of children raising children is precarious, since the youngest child in most any adult unsupervised large group of children will always be the easiest target to victimize, the target for violence, control and perverse entertainment within the hierarchy of this sort of group. Older children will not want to play with the younger children and ultimately they will reject and abandon him or her.

In the case with the child with the mosquito bites and sunburn, the other children ditched him after a short while and left him on his own for the rest of the day with no supervision.

Additionally, at the common age of three the parents with children in my center started looking to place their children into large institutionalized centers or Head Start. Too often the children's learned behavior that was acceptable at home and from their unsupervised social groups, resulted in their inability to form a relationship with another child or adult without becoming confrontational.

I witnessed this identical behavior with a few of the enrolled children at a private center that I was employed at. Two of the children had developed serious violent behavioral and social problems at ages three and four. They had been enrolled at the center since they were newborns. The seasoned teachers and director at the center could not understand or manage these severe cases.

The teachers were mystified and perplexed as to the source of where and what was occurring with these few children and why at the ages of three and four.

For more than a decade I had witnessed and experienced this unique phenomenon while working with children with this form of particular violent behavior. It comes from the extended family home and social environment. This includes the multi–generational family's social dynamics in relation to by whom and how the child was raised in the hierarchy. It involves children raising children in small or large groups at a young age with no adult supervision or interaction. In one out of two of these cases, I told one teacher what it was and where it came from. The teacher could not hear what was being said, as she adamantly defended the parents coming from a respectable multi–generational family in the community.

Between the ages of three to four and sometimes older I witnessed this change in some of the children in my center no matter what the circumstances were in relation to my one–on–one work with the children. This innocence lost and violent confrontational behavior contradicted the natural stages of early childhood human development. Emotional deprivation and trauma at a young age has a variety of ways of rearing its head with young children.

I will always have the vivid memories of this phenomenon occurring specifically with one child who had been enrolled in my center since he was six–weeks–old. On one day there could be seen a natural pure innate innocence, curiosity and intelligence as he tried to touch dust particles reflected in light and floating in a small sunbeam across the room. A couple of months later I would see the light in his eyes and his behavior change drastically to include deviance and violence combined with a heaviness and coldness in his being. I saw the pure innocence and intelligence of a child taken from his soul and what was left was a destructive anger and blankness. He was four–years–old.

Many parents in my center believed that with their children attending school at an early age it would make their children into geniuses. The words genius and smart were words I heard very often from the parents when describing their children and repeated by the children to describe themselves to me.

During the same time the words retard, dummy and stupid were also repeatedly told to the children from the parents and relatives. These words were commonly used in the home and the children would repeat them to each other endlessly consequently resulting in narcissism and bullying combined as one.

In one case I attempted to teach a child at age eight who could not read a clock or tell time. She could not do basic addition and subtraction with two or more place values. To teach a young child who had already been programmed to believe that they were a genius and had passed from one grade onto the next in public school, created a profound challenge for me.

To the children and adults, a mother is a title only. She was a female that procreated and then gave her children to others to teach and raise. She made money and bought the children things and financially supported the family. These women were almost always absent from their children's daily life due to work and personal social choices.

All of the children in my center were moved about from house to house, relative to relative, acquaintances or friends. The children had no consistent schedules, no structured home life, and they always returned to the child day care center physiologically and psychologically fragmented.

Each new week I had to start from the beginning by first observing, assessing and then meeting their individual basic needs. They were tired, hungry, and their behavior had changed back to what was expected and accepted at their home and social environment.

Too many of the children returned to my center with marks, scars and other injuries on their bodies from careless behavior. This was directly related to limited or no adult supervision while at home with their parents, extended family members or while placed in groups with other children unsupervised.

Working with these children made me realize for the first time of the high number of children in the U.S. who have no parents. This phenomenon is multi–generational and continues to escalate in families from all different social–economic backgrounds. The children had multitudes of guardians who let them do whatever they wanted to do with no guidance or repercussions.

In one case the grandparents who helped raise their grandchildren asked the children what they wanted to eat for dinner, they said they wanted donuts. The grandparents went to the store and bought the children donuts for dinner because that is what they wanted.

The biological mothers and fathers were physically absent from their children's daily lives. The parents were also emotionally unavailable for their children. This is an old phenomenon in this U.S. The difference between the past and now is that this form of non–parenting has risen to soaring new numbers.

In one case a child who was age four, was eventually placed in the care of his father. The child told me with glee that since he now lived with his father he could do anything he wanted. The father's own mother had left him and his father. His father told him at the age of five that he could do anything that he wanted to as long as he didn't get into trouble. He was raised with no parental supervision, nurturing, or guidance. When he became a young adult he ended up living on the streets and later fathered the child mentioned above.

Plant a Seed

The open minded humanity of my approach by working with parents as an educator required that the parent and I both accept full responsibility for the caring and education of their children. Most parents found it hard to accept responsibility for their children, preferring to hold others responsible and to adopt a passive or dependent attitude to the child day care center or school that their children attended. This has to change if the work with parents and children is to ever progress.

My objective was to encourage a creative relationship to both the child and parent as a whole. The dialectical mutuality between equals was designed to heighten the sense of responsibility in a parent for their own child's process of growth. I believed I was working on a shared task, to discourage reliance on the child day care center and to encourage reliance on the parent. It would help prevent exhaustion that can easily afflict hard working educators and to insure against their work becoming routine or lifeless.

This ideal is such that parents need to establish with an educator a working relationship through which they can conceive themselves as capable of sustaining a lasting bond of intimacy and trust. Only when this has been achieved can parents and children benefit from the kind of work with the children that educators regard as the crux of a supportive and nurturing educational environment for the young child.

Letting go meant that I had to remind myself that these multitudes of children were not mine. After working for more than a decade in the early childhood education and child care field I was financially ruined and exhausted. I closed my child day care center.

Study the Blueprint

When a child grows up spoiled, indulged, with no discipline or consequences for bad behavior and the child's ego is inflated, then as an adult when they want something it will usually result in a deviant or criminal act. They do it because their psyche has been groomed and taught that they can do whatever they want with no consequences and they can have anything they want because of their inflated ego.

A child that receives limited or no nurturing in an unstructured home life and when that home is filled with chaos and unpredictability, that child becomes part of an unnatural order. The natural state for a child to thrive and grow in is one of nurturing, a sense of security, intimacy, structure, stability and knowing what to expect next.

87

The child who grows up lacking what is natural will attempt to overcompensate when they are older in their relationships with others by an overwhelming desire to control every facet of that relationship and the other person in the relationship.

This type of altered need to control others can take on the forms of violence, verbal assault and malicious behavior. Because the un–nurtured child has become an adult there is a need for the child who missed the crucial developmental stages during the most important years of their childhood to return.

Within the framework of this individual they will grow into someone who seeks an uncontrollable need for order in their own life. They will compensate for this unmet need in childhood through unnatural acts of deviance, violence, obsession, lack of intimacy or disrespect and calculated domination of others during their adult life.

The most important shift in the human consciousness is the will to control and power, mastery and conquest—this is what gained dominance in our cultural history.

Humanity cannot be taught to children whose main objective and reward are possessions, privilege and dominance in a culture that insidiously takes over and ultimately destroys the essence of innate human development.

When children's developmental emotional needs are not met, this type of cultural phenomenon breeds inhumanity and the cycle of violence becomes endless in every facet within the adult society way of life. Social responsibility requires a person to have a conscience and to become consciously aware of their environment and actions.

In a consciously aware society the true intention is to evolve and create a progressively mature social intelligence. In order to attain this type of intelligence, the cultural environment requires children to be nurtured. Children need to be raised in safe and healthy surroundings in order for them to be consciously aware to feel and to have their feelings validated on an individual basis. Validation empowers the child.

This early childhood developmental human need has to be met in order for the child to grow into an adult capable of empathy. A culture without empathy is an immature society void of intelligence. The question that remains who is raising the children?

FERPA

Request for Permission Required

The Family Education Rights and Privacy Act (FERPA) of 1974 (20 U.S.C.S 1232g; 34 CFR Part 99) is a federal statute. The purposes of FERPA are to ensure that parents have access to their children's educational records. Additionally, the statute was passed to protect the privacy rights of parents and children by limiting access to these records without parental consent. For a more in–depth look at FERPA and its impact on Information Sharing and the Family Educational Rights and Privacy Act (FS–9639) go to the U.S. government's information website.

The federal guidelines provide that state government educational departments and institutions that receive funding under a program administered by the U. S. Department of Education must provide some control over the disclosure of information from student records. Disclosure means to permit access to or the release, transfer, or other communication of personally identifiable information contained in education records by any means, including oral, written, or electronic means, to any party except the party identified as the party that provided or created the record.

One day a state agency responsible for governing regulated child day care centers created a new regulation. The new regulation mandated that all regulated child day care center proprietors—home and group child day care centers who also home schooled were required to transfer and submit their children's home schooling records in their entirety from the Board of Education Department to the child day care administrative licensing unit.

Any and all licensors were given the authority and task to view and assess all of the family and student's personal records filed with the Home Schooling Office at the Board of Education Department. Both are separate government agencies under different government jurisdictions.

The child day care supervising unit's employees are not and never will consist of state certified educators. The licensors who work at the child day care unit are assigned to individual regulated child day care centers and are not mandated to have a prior formal education or experience in the areas of early childhood development and behaviorism, child care or education. A teacher with state certification does not by design qualify them as trained, experienced, or skilled in home schooling.

Home schooling is a very highly selective field of education that is regulated by an exclusively assigned office at the Board of Education Department. Refer to the chapter, "A Licensor" with the subheading, "Follow the Regulatory Trail."

Return to the New Normal

Some believe the first documented example of home schooling was with Alexander the Great being taught at home by Aristotle more than 2500 years ago. All children were home schooled in—academics, skilled trades or apprenticeships in the U.S. up until the late nineteenth century when state legislation was passed encouraging parents to send their children to public schools.

Abraham Lincoln was home schooled by his mother. Agatha Christie was home schooled by her mother. Alexander Graham Bell was home schooled by his mother. The list of famous people who were home schooled throughout the centuries is very long. The children Jaden and Willow Smith are home-schooled. Darrell Waltrip 3x-NASCAR Cup Series winner grew up being home-schooled. Poet Robert Frost 4x-Pulitzer Prize winner was home-schooled.

This list continues to grow because home schooling is taking place today and will always be present in the U.S. Home schooling is a parental right for all parents. This is a guaranteed protection under the First and Fourteenth Amendments of the U.S. Constitution.

The movement away from public schools and back to home schooling began in the 1960's by three significant people. One of whom is John Holt, Cambridge, MA. He saw the public school's system based on authoritarianism, structured sameness in curriculum and constricted schedules, contradicted the child's natural curiosity and ability to learn. The public school's method of teaching crushes the child's spirit and does not encourage it to grow in a natural state.

Public schools fail and will continue to fail because the educational system cannot provide an adequate quality of teaching in an environment that is safe and secure that encourages all children to learn. Homeschooling allows for customizing curriculum to the individual child's personality.

In home schooling you live and learn together as a family pursuing questions and interests as they arise and using conventional schooling on an "on demand" basis, if at all. John Holt started the magazine, *Growing Without Schooling* in August, 1977, making it the first magazine about home schooling in the U.S. Holt's only book about home schooling, *Teach Your Own* came out in 1981. It was revised by Holt's colleague, Patrick Farenga, and published in 2003 by Perseus Books.

John Holt died on September 14, 1985. *Learning All the Time* was left unfinished at the moment of Holt's death. The book was completed using materials he wrote for *Growing Without Schooling* and published in 1989. These references may be found at www.holtgws.com.

In my case the local Board of Education Department had an established Home Schooling Office that was accountable for registration, monitoring, approving curriculums, reviewing student's quarterly reports, testing and providing parent support on the subject matter. The succession of directors that supervised the Home Schooling Office had been well educated, experienced and were very passionate in guiding and supporting home schooling parents.

For the first ten years semi–retired public school principals held the director's position in the Home Schooling Office. The directors had knowledge of the diverse methods used in home schooling. They had extensive hands–on experience and understanding of what worked and didn't work in schools and with teaching children.

They were well seasoned veterans of the educational system and were enthusiastic about the selective field of home schooling. They believed in their job that they were doing. At the time the directors were very involved, extremely committed and took the civil servant's position to heart. This passion for their work extended itself to the point where they gave their home phone numbers to parents telling them to call them in case they had any questions or concerns.

In contrast the climate in the general public was increasing with anti–home schooling rhetoric and hostility. In particular, on the part of the sensationalized stories by the media that disseminated home schooling in the eyes of the wider public. Home schooled families faced extreme hostility, discrimination and were misunderstood. The general public felt that their point of view had a special significance and merit in this personal choice and private family matter on education.

During one year a new state educational regulation for home schooled student testing was passed. It eliminated the previous choice of a parent's right to directly administer the school tests to their children and required home schooled students to be tested on–site with other public school students in the Spring as a group in public schools.

The home schooling director in office at that time received a flood of phone calls from parents. The ramifications of the new regulation if allowed would be unconscionable and irreparable for home schooled children. The director knew this when the new regulation was passed and before the phone calls started coming into his office. I was one of the parents that called him.

What was obvious to the director and the parents was that mandatory on–site school testing would create false student test scores, label children inaccurately, create irreversible trauma by placing a child in an unfamiliar environment while ordering them to perform within an unknown group and with an unfamiliar adult. The new testing regulation contradicted the entire practice of home schooling that included creating a safe and nurturing natural environment for the child to learn and emotionally develop in.

Testing by public schools is specifically used as a form of volume control and schools are rewarded or punished with government funding based on those test scores. Teachers are rewarded or punished by classroom student test scores. Students are rewarded or punished for their individual test scores.

It is similar to a food chain but in reverse. Books by the volumes have been written on the subject matter. This commodity type scheme behind school testing is common knowledge in the education industry.

On the subject of testing, most home schooling parents know what their children know or don't know and should know because they are teaching their children one–on–one. Consequently, for most home schooling parents, tests have no priority or importance when home schooling children. The exception to this rule is the home schooling parent who is teaching from store bought curriculum and they believe in tests, rewards and punishments, whereby mimicking the public and private schools' teaching methods.

The home schooling director at the Board of Education Department overruled the new state regulation for mandatory on-site testing. He made his decisions on a case by case basis. He allowed or reinstated the parent's right to administer their children's tests at home. This is what I had previously done with my children and continued to do.

Each of the home schooling directors that I had experience with were loyal to the core philosophy of home schooling and educating children. They stood steadfast and true to the very end in their convictions when it came to acting as advocates for the education and rights of home schooled children and their parents. Their professional mandate included what was in the best interest of the development and education of children.

It was not a state's right to dictate and implement contradictory polices in terms of education for home schooled children and their parents. The reason behind the new regulation was that the state's education department had a desire to control across the board the diversities in home schooling families-to group them as one. The state government wanted all home schooling families to conform as a group to meet the state's education department's selective design or current administrator's mark.

At the local Board of Education Department, one home schooling director after another succumbed to heart failure or a stroke while working in the position at the Home Schooling Office. They had literally put their hearts and souls into their jobs. After the untimely death of the last home schooling director, there was a change in administration.

The Home Schooling Office at the Board of Education Department was revised. The new director was worlds apart from her successors in terms of knowledge and experience in home schooling. This included management operations and administration of the department.

She was allocated an additional budget to hire more clerical staff. At first I received frequent letters from the new director condemning, threatening, and stating that I had failed to send in my proposed curriculum and that my children were to be removed from the home schooling program. I also received numerous letters, stating that I had failed to properly file my quarterly reports on time and that my children were to be reported to a truancy officer as they were to be removed from the home schooling program.

When my children reached the ages of 18 to 24 and were both in college, the Home Schooling Office continued to mail thick manila envelopes at a cost of $4 and up per package to my home address. They contained dated materials required to be filled out to register my children and file my curriculums for the home schooling program.

The new director was not a hands–on home schooling director. The staff she hired was a reflection of herself. When she took over the position, for the first time in over ten years that my children had been registered with the program, I began mailing all documentation through certified mail with delivery confirmation. I made numerous calls to her office about the office's mistakes, false allegations and threats. Each time I was not allowed to speak with the new home schooling director directly but referred to her clerical staff who spoke with me.

I was told that the director wrote the cold letters personally addressed to all home schooling parents so that the parents who did not file their documents on time would and that I should ignore the letters because I was in compliance. The director's unprofessional actions created a bullying culture directed at homeschooling parents and children.

When I called about the mailing of application packages to my children, after the age of 18- when they were no longer in the program, the staff workers said they would remove my children's and my name from the files and mailing lists. They never did. I stopped calling.

The new home schooling director's type of academic administration consisted of an old archetype practiced in schools in order for volume control and applied to children in the classrooms. It starts by targeting the group as a whole, not the individual and then by instilling fear by using threats with accusations resulting in punishment to dominate and have power over the all, the group.

The new director applied this method to adults, and the group was—home schooling parents. This sort of behavior practiced in the academic field destroys all tolerance and eliminates all mutual respect between all parties involved. It is old school. This behavioral educational method was and is widely practiced in the school systems in the U.S. for more than a century; it never changed in some school districts and states or by teachers and administrators.

The new director had previously been a school teacher. This was when she first applied this type of behavior, while teaching. It was accepted as normal behavior for discipline and teaching by her peers in the public school system. She climbed up the ladder in her career while being rewarded. The director turned the Home Schooling Office into the most common archaic way school teachers teach and taught children in the U.S. by instilling fear through violent behavior.

A new state standard for education was first proposed in the late twentieth century and included the Erik Erikson's Psychosocial Development Theory in state registered and licensed centers along with all public schools. The former school teacher now turned into the homeschooling director bypassed the educational workshops and mandatory college curriculum for a new state standard of education for all state educators.

It was sad to see all of the previous directors' years of hard work and dedication that they had built into the Home Schooling Office, to become critically condemned while being systematically and eventually destroyed.

During this time-line, I held my breath in the hope that my family would survive this new old type of hierarchy of bullying and abuse. I needed to endure a couple of more years before beginning the college application process for my children.

Outline the Collision Course

Some regulated family and group child day care centers include registered home schooling parents in numerous states across the U.S. My child day care center was open on Saturdays, weekday afternoons and evenings. This type of business schedule of hours kept my weekdays open for home schooling.

In theory home schooling is incorporated in the family 24/7—this is not literally. Some of the children enrolled in my child day care came from transient families. My business schedules were always changing without being given advance notice for either child enrollment or termination. A true educator knows that home schooling curriculums and child day care programs can complement and support each other.

One example would be the center's curriculum for yoga in the summer. My children had previously been taught yoga when they were younger. They also participated in yoga exercises as a group with the center's children who ranged from ages 2–year–olds and older. My children created a learning support system for the younger group and they practiced what they had previously learned. Yoga for beginner, moderate or advance moves was integrated when the children were ready to move on. There may be times of overlapping of teaching when all the children present benefit.

Normally each curriculum and program can work around the other during non–working hours or rest time. The state agency of regulators for child day care is not composed of present day hands–on educators. Nor do they have the educational capacity to understand John Holt's teaching method, it contradicts everything they were taught and think.

The state regulators are limited administrators and business planners for regulated centers. Each year the overseeing state government agency responsible for the supervising child day care unit, ponders how to add to the state regulation sheets—book. This sometimes creates new, unrealistic or flawed state regulations for regulated and non–regulated child day care.

Repeatedly lead teachers and directors step down from their positions because of the insatiable demands of the mounting regulation sheets that they are responsible for in the classrooms and centers. This form of overzealous paper pushing and out–of–control record keeping circumvents the educator's original reasons for entering the profession. Though, it does support volume control of large numbers of children grouped together.

In this case it involved the state agency creating a new regulation targeted at home schooling parents who were group or family center proprietors. This new regulation mandated that all registered students submit entirely their private school records filed with the school district for children enrolled in the home schooling program to be viewed openly by licensors and other administrative employees in the child day care units across the state.

At the time of this new regulation the Board of Education Department's home schooling director made it clear to me that state and county agencies were in violation of the Family Educational Rights and Privacy Act (FERPA) under the U.S. Department of Education's Family Policy Compliance Office. In compliance with FERPA, no home schooling parent had to disclose any information from their children's student school records on file at the Board of Education Department to another government agency.

Additionally, the Board of Education Department would not release any home schooling student records to another government agency without that other agency meeting all the required conditions under FERPA. The state and county agencies that regulate and enforce child day care center regulations had not met the conditions to mandate disclosure of home schooling records from parents who were registered in the state to operate child day care centers.

Not only were the rights of home schooling parents being violated, but the state and county government agencies were in violation of FERPA. Noncompliance with FERPA can result in the loss of education grants and funds to the state from the federal government.

Home schooling is a very diverse area of specialized education. How and what individual families choose to teach is filed with the Home Schooling Office at the Board of Education Department because it is under their jurisdiction and their approval. I chose not to share my children's private student school records with the child day care unit. The new regulation passed by the state government had repercussions. Failure to comply with the new regulation was grounds for denial to renew my child day care center's state registration.

The home schooling director at the time offered to handle this matter directly with the child day care unit's director. I thanked him and then declined his offer thinking that I could handle the matter without any problem. I informed the licensor's unit that the new regulation was in violation of FERPA. As a courtesy to the unit I offered to provide only pertinent home schooling information to their office. This meant only the scheduled hours when I home schooled and what hours my child day care center was open. I declined to disclose any other private student home schooling files including my children's personal information, personal school curriculums, reports and test scores.

One day two licensors came to my child day care center. In retrospect, what if I had accepted the home schooling director's offer to allow him to deal directly with the child day care unit's director? Would the licensors' employed retaliation tactics of bullying, shaming, instilling fear and violence have entered my home and center that unforgettable autumn day?

Graduate to the Next Level

When people asked why I choose to home school, the answer was always the same. I could do a better job than what was available to my children at the time. What I did not share with people, was my decision to home school was based on pure instinct. It was a strong gut feeling and intuition that home schooling was the right choice for my children.

Sometime later the Colfax's gave a live television interview about home schooling. Soon after, I read their book, *Homeschooling for Excellence* by David Colfax, Micki Colfax. Their point was to inform parents to take responsibility for their children's education, stop blaming and relying on others to do it. Their book led to John Holt in Cambridge, MA and his support team for home schooling through the magazine, *Growing Without Schooling*.

The method used for home schooling my two children was moving away from a structured system of learning. The attention was concentrated on assisting my children to learn by focusing on their individual and natural sense of curiosity. They were being taught how to learn, and this included without material rewards or grades.

The home schooling schedule created was totally flexible on a daily need to need basis. The original Home Schooling Office's directors supported my method and curriculum on teaching, this was without debate and included John Holt's method for home schooling that the directors were familiar with.

The new contradictory and controversial government regulations, from the state Board of Education Department and the overseeing state agency for regulated child day care centers challenged home schooling and the parents who were teaching their children. Fixated state planners undermined the quality of education for all children in an environment that was safe and secure, and encouraging children to learn based on children's individuality.

As is true in everyone's educational growth, early childhood education becomes the building blocks of student's learning, thinking and behavior in their secondary years of schooling. These pieces fit together in a mosaic. The teaching curriculums and methods allow each student unique experiences combined with a progressive and contemporary academic education connected with the added emphasize on the emotional development needs of the human self. The home environment plants the seeds for self–starters and independent students who love to learn. The students learn in a natural setting.

Standardized tests are not a strong predictor of a student's success or of a student's success in college. Given that my children were home schooled, the college admissions process could not begin without the SAT or ACT test scores. A General Educational Development (GED) was not necessary to apply to colleges but was mandatory upon entering college when qualifying for financial aid. The GED has two stages for their testing. In the first step the student has to complete and pass a two day Predictor Test. This is followed by two days of testing for the GED.

Most colleges require a GED before the student's enrollment into their college and not the presumed acceptance date. Free Application for Federal Student Aid (FAFSA) along with other financial aid makes the same requirement for having the GED. These guidelines may continue to change over time.

Many colleges desire home schooled students. The required supporting documentation in the application process for home schooled students encompasses a vast amount of additional letters, curriculum records, descriptive writing and other papers to formulate and present the educational background of the home schooled student to the colleges. The home schooled student is submitting no school grades or grade point average to the college admission boards.

Each college has different requirements for the application process of admissions for home schooled students. The federal and state governments' educational statistics listing for the average scores projected for students from my children's socio–economic background proved to be incorrect. The evidence was reflected in their scores.

The first on–site school test administered to my children was the SAT. One son scored better than 76% of the National Group of College Bound Seniors and scored better than 79% of the State Group for College Bound Seniors. Another son scored better than 82% of the National Group of College Bound Seniors and scored better than 84% of the State Group for College Bound Seniors.

Genuine thanks goes out to the Home Schooling Office directors at the Board of Education Department who continually protected and fought for my family's educational rights and privacy when numerous state government agencies and civil servants attempted to harm the teaching, education, child emotional developmental needs, and the safety & welfare of my children.

Thanks goes to the home schooling director who protected my children's school records from disclosure to another government agency as that other state agency failed to meet the criteria for disclosure under FERPA when mandated by a new state regulation. As well as the home schooling director who used his executive decision to permit the parent/teacher to administer testing for my children in the home and not at the state mandated public school test sites.

These rare well experienced and educated civil servants stood up and chose to do the right thing at a time when other state government agencies and civil servants had consistently crossed the line.

To home school is a very personal and private decision. It is innate and a natural commitment that a parent—usually the mother and in some cases the father or other legal guardian—chooses to make for their children and family. It is not only what children are taught but how they are treated that determines the sort of adults they will become, paralleled by social and intelligence development in a natural environment.

Definitions

Mother's Helper

A Mother's Helper tends to be younger, between the ages of 17 – 21 and lacks the more specialized training of a nanny. Mother's Helpers generally work up to 45 hours per week. While they may do some light housekeeping, their focus is working with the children.

At seventeen I was employed as a mother's helper during the weekends and summer in the Berkshires. The family's main home was in Manhattan where we traveled to and from the Berkshires. My original responsibilities were to care for the three children for $50 a day. In time I was asked to do the laundry, light housekeeping, then eventually cooking and baking from recipes requested by the mother.

One day the parent's seven–year–old son warned me that if I did not do what he wanted me to do, he would tell his mother to fire me and that she would do it. I told the boy's mother of the conversation I had with her son. I requested to be paid $75 a day. I continued to work for the family until the end of the summer. The moral of the story is when seven–year–old children threaten caregivers and the parents continue to add more work duties to the care giver's daily tasks, then it is time to leave.

Au Pair

An au pair is usually between the ages of 18 and 26 years old and are typically in search of a new cultural experience while also desiring to serve as an integral part of a parenting team. The experience usually draws au pairs to improve on their foreign language skills. An au pair is not considered a domestic employee in Europe and therefore taxes need not be paid as such. Compared to the United States, European countries tend to pay far less for au pairs, nannies, caregivers and house help. This rule of thumb may change on a case to case basis.

European families often want American and English girls to work as au pairs in order to teach their children English. American families want European girls as au pairs for the similar reason of teaching their children another language. The word Au Pair is a French term, which means on par or equal to. This term indicates the caregiver is living on an equal basis in a reciprocal, caring relationship between the host family and the children. They will typically be a young woman or sometimes a young man from a foreign country that chooses to help look after the children and provide light housekeeping. The au pair is given room and board and is typically paid a weekly sum of pocket–money as a wage and generally stay with their host family for one year.

When I was eighteen–years–old I worked as an au pair in Florence, Italy. Local families listed jobs openings for au pairs at the U.S. Consulate General Florence—Italy. Working and living as an au pair with an Italian family paid a salary of fifty dollars a week with Sundays and some Saturdays off. The family I lived with had three children.

At that time the family's house was being renovated and this meant sharing the younger children's bedroom in an apartment until the renovation on the main house had been completed. The job responsibilities involved caring for the children, answering the door and phone. There were no housekeeping responsibilities required. I discovered in time that in a Roman Catholic country everything was closed on Sundays with the exception of the church.

My au pair position ended approximately the same time that I could understand spoken Italian and had acquired a new appreciation for Italian fresh made cheeses. After a few months of working as an au pair, I was home sick and returned to the U.S.

Nanny and Manny

Nanny Agencies are located by geographic areas in the U.S. Some cities and areas are not represented by nanny agencies. Other cities have large clusters of nanny agencies. Live–in or live–out is a choice that parents looking for a nanny must decide. Some parents have no preference on this option when looking for a nanny.

The rule of thumb for a live–in nanny is a weekly salary for employment of 40–50 hours and a car made available for the nanny. Any hours worked over the set hours are to be compensated. Live–out nannies work 40 hours or less in a week. When the hours include more than over 40 hours, they will need to be compensated. Unemployment taxes and other federal withholding taxes are the responsibility of the family who are the employers. Health Insurance coverage is optional and with the new health-care laws may create additional choices. Some nanny agencies offer a payroll service to families for a fee.

Agencies located in a particular city will place live–out nannies only from that area. This means do not expect an agency to place a nanny as a live–out in Boston if you live in Baltimore. If a nanny is a live–in, agencies won't place a nanny if they have children and/or a husband with the anticipation to live on the property.

As a result of not having access to an agency, nannies looking for work may use the public referral service listings on-line. This makes the search very difficult because almost anything goes as far as listed demands and expectations from both parties involved. Many times parents say they want one thing and in truth they don't know what they want.

Agencies acting as the go between of employer and employee will sift through this lack of communication. Many of the Internet job boards have grouped these positions—mother's helper, nanny, au pair, and babysitters—together in the attempt of matching families with child care. This type of generalizing only compounds the confusion more with parents who are new to the child care market and have preconceived ideas that come along with the job titles.

At nanny agency websites the potential nannies list their bios and families list what they are looking for and what they expect to pay. Both hope for a match. The membership listing fees at some job board websites usually is paid by the family who is searching. In some cases, the nanny also pays a membership fee.

The term nanny had been overused and misused by Americans since the mid–twentieth century and up to the present at a time when many mothers are no longer raising their children. Private agencies usually define nannies as more mature, experienced and educated child care professionals, but it is no longer the absolute rule. The general public over time has placed all child caregivers into one group under the heading of nanny.

Today families are requesting young girls and sometimes require them to have some college or a college degree and little or no experience. For recent college graduates with a background in early childhood development and education, it is a second option to follow a career into the nanny field. An education in the field is not a guarantee that a nanny is qualified.

In one case a parent doctor team hired a college graduate with a degree in early childhood development and education. One day the parents discovered the nanny had given their one–year–old child popcorn to eat. On another occasion the nanny had given an age inappropriate toy as a gift to the child.

The nanny's poor judgment in terms of safety issues had taken its toll on the parents. The parents complained she had no common sense when it came to caring for their son and that her lack of better judgment was consistent over a span of ten months. They had invested thousands of dollars in fees through a nanny agency out–of–state to place her as a live–in with their family. The family was also from another state and under a two year employment contract while working in their professional positions. They dismissed the nanny after one year in their employment.

Internet job board listings for child caregivers that are open to the public generally mean the market's low–end in wages and services. In one case a mother was looking for a live–out nanny to care for her toddler.

The parent included in the advertisement that her son had broken his arm at a child day care center. Subsequently the mother removed her son from the center. The parent offered to pay $140 a week for full–time child care in her home stating that the dollar amount was what she had paid the child day care center. In this case, the wage the parent offered violated employment labor laws. No parent can compare in–home private child care to the same rate system under state regulated child day care centers. Refer to the chapter titled, "Rates" for more information.

Salary ranges for nannies are typically from minimum wage to $20 an hour depending on the region of the country you live in. A nanny may work anywhere from part–time a few hours a week or up to twelve hours a day. It depends on the needs of the family and whether it's a live–in or live–out arrangement. The number of children to be cared for is also a factor on how much is paid. In some households the family may employ two nannies to meet their children's needs and the family's afford-ability level.

In another case an advertisement listed an open position for a child care professional. The requirements for the position included a polished professional to care for two children. They had to engage the children in fun, creative and safe play while incorporating educational activities and guiding the children to independence. They also had to nurture the children into creative thinkers and help form the children into the kind of loving, happy, caring individuals the world needs. The child care professional had to appreciate the value of education, tutor the children, and assist with homework and music lessons. Most importantly, they had to be extremely responsible and possess unwavering integrity. The family stated that they were warm, loving, kind, outdoorsy and creative. The position required someone to be flexible and on call for the family and possible travel.

I had found the above advertisement peculiar and at the same time ironic, as the specific qualities required for child care reflected those found in an educated full–time mother who chooses to start a family and to raise her children. Basically the ad was advertising for the position of a full–time mother. This parent who placed the advert was occupied with other commitments and could not fill the position herself. Why did she choose to have children if she planned to give them away to be raised by another individual who imitated an idealistic duplicate of a mother?

The career in child care typically hires an underpaid group of mostly women, young students and in some cases men in today's U.S. culture. There is a high demand to fill the vacancy that was once a mother's unpaid full–time work.

There are law requirements when employing in–home private child care. When you have someone care for children in your own home you must pay your in–home child care provider no less than minimum wage. The wage would be the state or federal minimum wage for the first forty hours, time and one half after forty hours.

The employer of an in–home child caregiver is responsible for reporting and paying Federal Income Taxes (FIT). For more information of the FIT rate, forms, filing procedures, and general assistance, you may contact the Internal Revenue Service. As an employer, you are required to file Federal Unemployment Tax (FUTA). For more information on the FUTA rate, forms, filing procedures and general assistance, you may contact the nearest IRS office. For more information, contact the nearest Unemployment Office. When an in–home child caregiver works 40 or more hours per week, you are responsible for providing Worker's Compensation coverage. The insurance may be purchased from any private company licensed to write such coverage from the State Insurance Fund. For more information, contact the nearest office of the Workers Compensation Board. When an in–home child caregiver works 40 or more hours per week, you are responsible for providing Disability Benefits Insurance. When hiring any child caregiver in the home the laws will change and it is the parents' responsibility to keep aware of these changes as an employer.

Some parents who search for child caregivers, whether it is for a nanny, au pair or babysitter to work in their home, believe it is an inexpensive means to an end. By this way the parents avoid tuition costs, including paid vacation and paid sick days paid to child day care centers or preschools. This way of thinking in some cases is a mistaken belief.

In–home child caregivers under law have to be paid hourly. In a regulated child day care center a full–time day rate is based on six hours or more for a full day rate. The full–time rate reflects the child day care center or preschool contract. In contrast if the family has three children it may be less expensive to hire a full–time nanny then to place the three children in a child day care center.

Nanny vs. Housekeeper

Nannies are primarily for teaching, caring and nurturing children. When duties such as house cleaning, pet care, family laundry and meals become inclusive in the job description then it is obvious the parents are looking for a housekeeper and not a nanny. Yet many mothers and fathers see it as all one job and use the distinguished title of nanny when the position is actually a housekeeper.

This American cultural phenomenon is rooted in the need to make an impression of privilege and validate a higher social status for the family than what is real. What is considered women's work—cooking, child care and other domestic duties in the household—continually is demeaned by men and women who are no longer coupled to this form of work as they announce to people that they employ a maid or nanny. While the truth is they have hired a cleaning woman, babysitter or an uneducated domestic worker who most often are paid a fraction of what the above titled two positions would be paid.

The private nanny agencies more often than not are a better way to go for both families and nannies looking for a match. The agency's fee required from the parents usually includes guaranteed stipulations if things don't work out. This is not an exclusive rule with all agencies. The mutual business arrangement when going through a private nanny agency will bring both the family and nanny to be independently interviewed by the agency. Most of the time this includes a background check and possible other certifications required by the agency before families are introduced to potential nannies for placement in their homes.

Regulated Child Day Care Center

Throughout this book I use the general U.S. media terminology child day care center when addressing all three types of regulated child day care for children. These include: registered family child day care, registered group child day care and licensed child day care centers. Many nonprofit child day care organizations started the movement for modification of the regulatory term of day care to be changed to child day care when addressing regulated child day care. Many people working in the profession felt it was necessary to bring clarity between adult day care and child day care.

The following terms are important for parents to understand. They may find the definitions under their individual state's regulation sheets for regulated and informal child day care. In many states the regulation sheets may be found under the Office of Children & Family Services. Each state in the US. has differing and similar laws and regulations concerning child day care. The following terms and their definitions may not apply to every state:

Child Day Care Provider, Operator, Child Day Care Center, Family Day Care Home, Group Family Day Care Home, License, Registration, Applicant, Staff, Director, Child Day Care, Child Day Care Center Director, Day Care Center, Group or Family Child Care Provider, An Informal Provider

A parent under state regulations has the right to view and have access to all state child day care regulations. In one state the accepted regulation for teacher to child ratio guidelines is one teacher to ten children in a licensed center's room for children four–years–old. In another state the accepted regulation for teacher to child ratio guidelines may be different for the same age group in a center's room. As the ages of the children regress the ratio of children per teacher also changes.

When a center has accreditation from one of various independent child care or educational organizations in the U.S., guidelines may require that specific center to have a lower teacher to child ratio in addition to other standards than state regulations.

Infant means a child up to 18 months of age.

Toddler means a child 18 months to 36 months of age.

Older Toddler means a child between the ages of 24 and 30 months to 35 months

Preschooler means a child who is at least 3–years–old through 5–years–old

and who is not yet enrolled in kindergarten or a higher grade.

Kindergartener means a child who is attending private or public kindergarten usually 5–years–old

School–aged child means a child attending first grade or beyond usually 6– years–old through 13–years–old

Regulations And Training

Enlighten Yourself

All operators, program directors, teachers and teacher assistants for licensed and registered child day care centers, school–aged child day care programs, group child day care and family child day care homes must have thirty hours of state approved curriculum of training every two years. Each new provider and alternate provider must complete a minimum of fifteen hours of training during the first six months of registration.

Each state may have different requirements and regulations. Training will change over time. Regulation training usually addresses the following topics:

1) Principles of childhood development, including the appropriate supervision of children, meeting the needs of children enrolled in the program with physical or emotional challenges and behavior management and discipline
2) Nutrition and health needs of children
3) Child day care program development
4) Safety and security procedures, including communication between staff and parents
5) Business record maintenance and management
6) Child abuse and maltreatment identification and prevention
7) Statutes and regulations pertaining to child day care and
8) Statutes and regulations pertaining to child abuse and maltreatment

Do the Equation

As the number of children enrolled into child day care centers change, the need for child day care workers can unpredictably change overnight as quickly as a parent being informed that they are laid off from their employment. An example of this is when the latest recession in the U.S. led to millions of people losing their employment. This had a domino effect on the enrollment numbers in child day care centers across the country.

Before the U.S. recession occurred, geographic pockets of economic changes were always taking place within family households. This affected centers without warning, staff lost their jobs and some centers went out of business. There is a high demand for low paid child care workers and babysitters, and they have entered the professional regulated child day care market.

Many individuals in this era of child care workers are a byproduct of multiple generations who were raised and cared by child care institutional settings, various caregivers or informal babysitters. This new generation of individuals who are mostly women and college graduates, entering the profession, often lack basic skills and common knowledge. This widespread problem originates from their childhood development and what is acceptable and non–acceptable when interacting and teaching young children.

State education and training requirements are based on child development, behavior, nutrition, preventing disease transmission and so on. Re–educating adults in the latter fields, when they have been taught and raised to think and interact in a dissimilar behavior, is a challenge. This frequent problem presents itself starting from the top to the bottom of a school's or center's hierarchy. It includes directors, principals, proprietors, lead teachers, teacher assistants and substitutes.

Regulated child day care centers' staff training has to be approved and recognized by the state and the government's supervising child day care unit who administer the state regulations. This does not stop numerous solicitors and marketers from other states and within the state from phoning and mailing literature about their training products for sale to regulated centers. Solicitors continually called my child day care center, asking me to purchase training materials they were offering. These materials did not meet the requirements set by the state for regulated child day care training. Solicitors further manipulated the government's "do not call list" law when calling family and group centers. Their first opening line that is said: "this is a business to business call".

In a licensed child day care center there may be offered in–house training by the directors, freelance instructors or other in–house staff. Usually the staff's paid training inside the child day care center takes place on a day when the facility is closed for vacation, during after work hours or at the time of the employee's break. The other choices are to enroll in training outside the facility.

When I worked at a high–end center, it was not the state that approved the training for the child day care staff. The director approved the staff training. They accepted most forms of training when it came from outside their facility, as long as it was vaguely related to the state's guidelines though it was not approved by the state. That was the standard the director held for teachers who previously had or were in the process of working towards earning a college degree. The director set different criteria for different staff in the center's employment.

Child advocacy organizations within and outside states will assist in providing and locating professional development through classes and training programs or by attending state educational conferences across the U.S. and college programs. Included will be workshops, classes, and video conferences, mandatory continual certification from the American Red Cross for Infant and Child First Aid, the American Heart Association for Infant and Child CPR and so on.

Watch Your Words: Little Ears Can Hear

Attending state approved educator workshops opposed to a center's in-house training, opens up a new window to what other educators are practicing. This may include a new state standard for education for state educators in early childhood development. Or it may introduce the personalized variety of early childhood teaching that is taking place across a state or the U.S. in any given regulated center or preschool.

At one state educational workshop that I attended, the topic was on patriotism, peace and preschool. During a group discussion a preschool teacher shared her approach she used for her class on the subject of September 11th. The teacher explained that she had said: "that group of bad men" when talking to her classroom of three and four–year–olds. What was obvious to some of the teachers in attendance at the workshop was missed by others in the room. The presenters who were state university professors at the workshop challenged the teacher on the words she had chosen when speaking to the children.

The words she had used reinforced to the young children, were gender and ethnically biased. As the discussion continued the presenters went further and tried to make clear to all of the teachers, the acceptable teaching practice for young children was not to tell children that people are bad but to explain to children some people do bad things.

The presenters were using a teaching ideology based on principles taught in religious institutions in the U.S. dating back to the 1960's. When a child hears those words they associate that all people are good. There is a backlash when teaching young children that people are not bad. It would be unconscionable to teach young children that all people are good and sometimes people do bad things. This type of religious dogma designed for young children incorporated that all people have good with in them. When placing a whole group—all people—into one distinct depiction while teaching children sets the framework for the abusers and their innocent victims within the group.

Listen Up

Under a state regulation for all regulated child day care centers a specific number of teachers are required to remain in the nap rooms at all times. The time period would encompass two hours for state regulation guidelines and up to an additional 45 minutes for processing and transitioning of the group.

When I worked at a center the conversing that took place among the teachers was nothing short of personal and center gossip. These conversations included the student teacher's weekend party with the police showing up at her home, different experiences she had babysitting for the center's families, how much they paid her and what the inside of their homes were like.

One teacher made derogative ethnic comments about one child's parents—who were first generation Americans—while he sat on his cot wide awake. Two senior teachers made degrading remarks about a three–year–old girl's parent's poor choices in purchasing their child's blanket and clothes. There was persistent maligning and malicious remarks made by teachers about other teachers who were not present at that specific moment in the nap rooms.

When a child is in different stages of sleep or not asleep, no matter what their ages are they can hear. Adult conversing can be heard and understood by young children. Degrading a child's parent–or a child–can have a profound effect on behavior and emotional development; ditto goes for when a parent degrades another parent within the ear shot of the child.

Watch Your Words: Big Ears Can Hear

A student teacher was enrolled at a state university for early childhood education. She also worked at a center. One day while in the staff's lounge she wanted to update the other teachers on what she had been taught the previous day at college. The classroom course study was on the subject of managing child behaviorism.

The student explained that the professor had taught her class that each culture is a determining factor on the child's behavior and has to be taken into account when understanding their behavior. She stated for example: "Native American children are taught to do everything perfect so if a teacher tells them to do something they won't do it if they cannot do it perfectly and the African American child grows up with a constant flow of relatives and people coming and going in their home…"

Please refer to the chapter, "A State Standard" with the subheading, "Return to Basics."

Another teacher and I were shocked and had heard enough from this student teacher when we both spoke up to tell her how inaccurate and bias that way of thinking was. The student teacher looked at the two of us as if we were both clueless and walked away. Her professor had taught her this misinformation the day before. He had won out in this case superseding two mature educators who had firsthand experience working with children from all cultural and economic backgrounds for more than two decades. Furthermore, I had been taught the same state mandatory course on the new state educational standard by a different teacher through a government program in a directly opposite format than what the college student was taught.

Additionally, at a state university's business class, a professor conveyed a story referring to her mulatto children. When I heard the word mulatto, I asked the student not to use that derogatory word. The student said: "No, it is fine to say the word mulatto because my college teacher had said it and she has been teaching for fifteen years." Mulatto is originally from the Spanish word that means mule. This term was used during slavery that referred to a child of a black person and a white person. In Colonial Latin America—Spanish and African people were denied basic political, economic, and social rights due to their mixed heritage. The definition for mule is the sterile offspring of a female horse and a male donkey, valued as a work animal, having strong muscles, a body shaped like a horse, and donkey like.

Almost forty–years ago I was taught at school in another state, that for more than two hundred years U.S. legislation and administrative agencies continued to define racial groups by using an out–of–date *law established more than three centuries ago originating from outside America*. Additionally, the U.S. government's archaic definition on racial grouping included: any in the least traceable African ancestry in the individual, including those with no phonotypical trace of ancestry, designates all those persons into the African American group.

111

The U.S. government's former use of this obsolete definition helped strengthen and intensify cultural prejudices among the White, Black, Hispanic and racially mixed American population. This contributed to a cultural system that survived the legal culture. The constitutional guarantee of equal protection under the law was designed to incorporate equality for all cultures and races. These American historical facts negate the U.S. government's definition of race and race groups. I would discover over the decades that my education differed greatly from the U.S. general population with how they had been educated and understood personal identity taught in the public schools and at home.

The out–dated definition for racial grouping is still in use today by most Americans in the U.S. When news media, educators, community leaders and government administrations apply it indifferently when speaking, their words show their educational roots. They are teaching and perpetuating racism from one generation to the next generation and this cycle becomes endless because they have the loudest voices in this country.

When the media recently reported a police shooting and death of a black unarmed student–accompanied along with his photograph on national news that was carried over into international news–I did not see a black young man. A couple of days after the tragedy, the mother of the young man was interviewed on CNN. The news commentator had changed the race group of the young man as no longer black but to interracial. The interview with the white mother about her son, proved the point of how absurd and ignorant race grouping is. When President Obama, before and at the beginning of his term, stood firm to his race identity as interracial or biracial, I was relieved to have a modern educated individual as president.

Obama soon afterwards surrendered to not fight the challenge of his group reclassification as black realizing it was a futile effort. Who can argue with Oprah and many other high profile public speakers when they cried and applauded publicly that the first black president had been elected? And then the international and global community followed suit contributing to perpetuating racism around the world while *they* reclassified Obama's race group.

These are only a few examples of what 'educators' are teaching young and adult students. It is an integral part of their personal educational roots and what they were taught to believe that is being introduced to new students in the schools and at home, and in the public mainstream generation after generation. To re–educate adults is often challenging and is usually improbable. To teach both gender and racial based ignorance in educational settings to young children and young adults who pass it on is unfathomable to all human intelligence.

A Child Day Care Center

Open a New Door

I was employed at a high–end licensed child day care center that had obtained elective accreditation. The center's goal was to become an accredited nursery school. On my first day of employment the director had asked me to bring my favorite book from my center to read to the children. I brought one of my favorite books, written by Lisa Jobe Carmack, *Philippe In Monet's Garden,* published by the Museum of Fine Arts in Boston. My first weeks working at the center were like a breath of fresh air. I felt invigorated and passionate again teaching.

Many of the enrolled children at the center had met the primary levels of Maslow's Hierarchy of Needs from their home environment. The seven human developmental needs listed in Maslow's Hierarchy are: Physiological, Safety, Belongingness and Love, Esteem, Cognitive, Aesthetic, and Self–actualization Needs. Most of the parents had taught their children well in relation to manners, respect, social skills and the ability to think and speak. Nearly every one of the children came to the center well rested, fed and clean.

In the outside sand box the conversation lead by three–year–old twins was about the hazards of SUVs to the environment. They told me that their mother had taught them this fact. A conversation led by another three–year–old was in reference to the outdoors in the Australian outback. The son and father had read books on the subject. They had also watched together the children's program on the Animal Planet Channel to extend the child's interests.

These principles and familial bonding came from the home. The parents had planted the seed in the children's mind that nature should be respected. Some three–year–old and four–year–old children would randomly run up to teachers to hug, kiss, hold hands or rest on a shoulder when they were read to. Many of the children had learned this accepted behavior from their home environment. Sometimes other children would mimic the other children. The fact for some of these children was that their social behavior was not genuine.

In the mix of all of these children there were the genuine, the imitators and the few mean aggressors. For a small group of the children violence, destruction, verbal and physical degradation and tormenting were a part of their normal social behavior in their daily routine. This could be traced directly back to their home environment and to the non–parenting parents.

Team teaching in the center numbered between two and five teachers to each classroom. That number depended on the number of children enrolled in a class by their age and if there were children with special needs. One classroom had four to five teachers to a ratio of fifteen children. Those five teachers were not in the room all of the time at the same time. This fact is important to know when parents are given child to teacher ratio guidelines.

As time passed my wide–eyed innocence and naiveté began to fade as I saw the daily reality taking place. The children in assigned rooms were not bonding with one or two adults as their primary caregivers but instead were exposed to an ever changing staff and to alternating part–time and full–time enrolled children. During the first months that I worked at the center, in one classroom alone, four staff members were transferred to another class or changed employment. The director moved teachers from classroom to classroom the way a valet parks cars in a parking lot from one spot to the next.

The classroom of three–year–old and four–year–old children confused the names of teachers. Some children would continually ask the lead teacher where the missing teachers had gone, as if a succession of mysterious deaths had occurred. These children did not respond well to new interactions with the ever occurring changes. Overall the children naturally placed all their demands, needs for attention and conversations with the one remaining lead teacher. They were familiar with her. The lead teacher was burning the candle at both ends.

The director had initiated these changes without taking into consideration the harmful fall out for both the children and the teachers in the classrooms. This type of academic administration contradicted Erik Erikson's Psychosocial Theory Stage One—the principles of brain development and relationships with other people early in life. Relationships are the major source of development of the emotional and social parts of the brain—this encompasses social trust and mistrust which depends on consistency and sameness of experience provided by a caregiver.

The child day care center did accept a small handful of scholarship and government subsidized enrolled children from households who could not afford the high tuition. These children started the enrollment process usually by a personal referral to the center's administrators.

Some children were enrolled part–time and attended the center two or more days a week. The part–time children were constantly confused to what day it was and to who the different children were, combined with the ever changing teachers and all of the other changes that transpired from day to day operations. Some of the children had a full–time stay at home parent, nanny or grandparents in their daily lives. In the majority of these cases the children came from a two parent working professional household with one or the other parent picking up their children after a six to eight hour day at the center. In very rare cases the child's day was nine hours enrolled at the center.

Typically, one or more parent had begun the process of teaching their children in the home from a very early age. This educational concept of adult lead creative play designed for young children was the similar method of teaching at the center. Learning through play and experiences with adult led interaction will result in young children doing extremely well in the three Rs even though the children are not being directly taught the three Rs.

Learning begins in the home and in this type of setting most of the children's learning skills were being reinforced in this center's educational approach that complimented the children's home environment.

Exam the Personal Signature

Directors or proprietors in each child day care center and early childhood program or nursery school, will have their own philosophy, management approach, style of program and mission statement. Teachers in each classroom will also bring into play their own personal style of teaching and interacting with young children.

At the unconscious level, both teachers and children are participating in what alchemists term as a coniunctio. Like two chemical substances, they are drawn together in the analytic situation by affinity. When two chemical substances combine both are altered. This is precisely what happens in transference. It is a unique recipe and each relationship brings about a different result. This process occurs on other subconscious and conscious levels as well.

Some teachers may see how certain children are drawn to each other or not drawn to each other. Sometimes both the children or only one child's identity and behavior will change. In a similar manner certain children are drawn to certain teachers and vice versa. It is an energy transference that takes place on different levels of the human psyche. It is a chemical process and alteration of each person.

In each recipe it formulates a new chemical product and outcome. Experienced teachers through observation see this process occur over and over throughout the years. This also occurs between adult educators in all educational facilities. In large educational environments it is more recognizable due to the high volume of children and adults pairing off or forming groups. One can observe the diverse effects based over time.

What Do You Believe

The center's unwritten policies included don't ask and don't tell. Teachers did not tell the parents about incidences when other children would hurt their child. One day a three–year–old child picked up a solid wooden chair, swung it, and intentionally struck the head of another child. The incident left a large welt and bruise on the smaller boy's forehead. This incident occurred more than once. On one of these occasions when the physical evidence could not be hidden the director instructed the student teacher to tell the parents that the child had hit his head on the chair. No senior or lead teacher would carry out this deed. This form of administration practice was repetitive where not accepting responsibility was a strategy to protect the group, academic team and the surrogate family aka the center.

One day during pick–up a mother confronted a teacher regarding what her 3–year–old son had told her. He had repeatedly gone home with urine on his clothes and his mother asked her son how it had happened. He told her that another boy had purposely urinated on him more than once in the bathroom. This had been witnessed by the teacher whom the mother was confronting as well as other teachers. The boy stood by his mother's side and watched as the teacher denied the incident ever happened.

To repeatedly falsely accuse a 3–year–old boy, almost four, for peeing on his clothes when the teacher knew he didn't, personally attacks the boy's credibility. When an adult/educator lies in front of a child and about the child, a pact has been created resulting in no value to the victim and this type of cancer will thrive and spread. This teacher was dependent on her employment. Teachers in general with low self-esteem and who did not have seniority in their teaching positions were more compliant for these types of parent and center public relation matters. In return it gave them employment security thereby being rewarded for protecting the team.

The aggressive child who was the perpetrator in this case had a long history of violent bullying behavior in the center. His strategies for building and defending his identity were to persecute and denigrate the teachers and children within his group to experience shame on a daily basis. He had an inflated sense of self-importance and lacked any empathy. Repeatedly he hit and threw toys at most all of the children and repeatedly hit very hard a few of the teachers on their buttocks, faces, and breasts.

One day after playing with his feces in the toilet, he took his soiled hand and smeared it on the lead teacher's face. He persecuted and degraded his victims daily by forcing them to experience shame and thereby made himself the winner at their expense.

The director of the center refused to terminate the child. This violent behavior had continued for more than one year. He stole from other children's cubbies, and lied to teachers and his mother when asked about the missing items. Later his mother brought back some stolen items to the center. His stealing continued. When he was taken for a second professional evaluation the final summary report proved inconclusive.

His constant aim was a winner loser dynamic and to prove he was the winner. With bullies there can only be one winner forcing everyone else to become the shame ridden looser, whether they are right or wrong the bully will always win. He had an inflated sense of self-importance from his family's ties within the community and consistently reinforced by the center's director, both of whom further validated that his worth was more than his victims. He was taught and groomed that he could do whatever he wanted and that is why he did it. Bullies do not come from happy homes, protected in their parents love and filled with a sense of their own self worth.

The violent behavior from the child was occurring daily as he manipulated and controlled all of those around him by means of deviance and violence. He had that all familiar look of a cold blankness in his eyes that I had seen before with other children while working for over a decade in my center. In the bathrooms he repeatedly targeted two boys by deliberately urinating on them. His goal was to degrade and shame others who were easy targets. This child was three–years–old and going on four.

Almost every day outside on the playground a few children purposely pushed other children down. One day a three–year–old child's head hit the path's pavement hard and bounced. No incident report was written up and nothing was said to the parents of either child. When I asked a senior teacher about writing a report I was told unless there was physical evidence of an injury to the child an incident report was not a mandatory policy. What I saw daily were contradictions of written policies that were tactics to consistently protect the team. It was ethically and professionally confounding to me.

The children's sense of a safe and secure environment to learn and play in did not exist. They were being taught daily to suppress their feelings and emotions. These children were being taught to not feel and/or to lack empathy. This type of behavior brings into play irreparable trust issues for children with adults. Communication between the child and parent is diminished by adult dishonest behavior. Had this center's director been trained in the new state standard for education?

The parents were not privy to the daily bullying and violent behavior that some of the children were experiencing and other children were witnessing. Or were they? Was it the parents' expected and accepted knowledge when putting children in large groups? Did the bullying culture infuse itself throughout the adult community?

On the subject of the children with serious behavioral problems, the director and the senior teachers contemplated strategies to control the uncontrollable bullying and violent behavior. The director then second guessed strategies and everyone had opinions. These inconsistencies when addressing the bullying and discipline added to the anarchy and escalated the children's violent behavior. Child termination due to bullying and mental health issues was not an option by the center's administration.

The director's belief is that the center was the only one to care for all of these children. This poor judgment and type of ideology may have been lost in good intentions. Or was her inflated self importance marked by a lack of empathy for the victims, part of the bullying culture and environment she had been raised and taught in. She set no limits in these types of relationships that she created for herself and for every one of the children. On a daily basis she justified that she loved all of the children and they all loved her and all the children loved each other.

This form of academic administration incorporated the director's personal signature and teaching philosophy at the center. This is not love. This is counter–productive teaching and child care for young children. Not one child–or teacher– should be sacrificed or suffer violence, shame and denigration, for the better good of one or for the all of the group.

Look at the Different Faces

At the center children were taught daily that they were all friends and a child who said otherwise was told repeatedly by the teachers that they were all friends. This led to unmerciful daily teasing from specific children telling other children that they were not their friends. This type of repeated behavior results in shaming and denigrating their victims in the group as the losers, depriving their target of social membership.

When a child spit, hit, grabbed or committed some other violent act upon another child, they were reminded that they were all friends and that was not acceptable behavior. This method of discipline did not curtail the violent behavior. The victimized children were instructed by the teachers to hug their abusers and the bullies were told to say they were sorry for what they had done. This did not stop the repeated offenses from the perpetrators towards their victims and they were not genuinely sorry because there can only be one winner, the bully. This one size fits all teaching approach taught the bullies to do whatever they wanted to do because they could.

For the victimized children this would reinforce the breach of their personal space and physical boundaries that their perpetrators had previously violated. Senior teachers instructed me to teach children to hug their abusers. I would and could not instruct a child to hug anyone under any circumstances unless they freely chose to do so by their own initiative.

There were a few incidences of teachers being violent. This sort of behavior usually involved pulling children's wrists and arms while simultaneously verbally disciplining them. It was rare among most teachers but it was a common behavior for a few of the teachers that I witnessed. It begins by instilling fear, threats, shaming and physical domination with the power to control.

I witnessed this behavior once with another center while they were taking a trip on the metro. It is a form of teacher discipline for volume control. This accepted behavior from these types of teachers is learned behavior prior to their working with young children.

In the case at this center two of these teachers were senior teachers and one was not. The director told me that the one teacher, who had been hired around the same time I had been, was hired specifically for her strong hand. The director was a former college professor at a state college in the Early Childhood Department.

Instilling fear, threats, shaming or using physical violence on young children—as well as adults—in order to control, denigrates the self and grooms the next generation to repeat the same. The personal signature of the center's director and some of the teachers when it came to education in early childhood development, teaching, behaviorism and discipline, was out–of–date and narcissistic.

That is how the environment was set–up. From early childhood to career level, bullying was established and accepted as the norm, it will continue with the future generations entering into the workforce.

There are some children who hit other children and some do not. Some children hit worse than others. Some teachers are very controlling or too rough. Some teachers may not understand or like a specific child and they would demonstrate this in their actions and words.

This interface meets at the unconscious level. Both teachers and children are two chemical substances when combined both are altered as they both participate in a coniunctio. The outcome may be a nonconstructive one or a constructive one. The end result is never the same for everyone.

The source of the violent behavior by the children was coming from their home environment. It became merged in multiplicity at the center. To encourage those few parents to take responsibility for their children's bad behavior was impossible in these cases. The parents were in denial and believed by placing their children in this high–end center with the other children it would resolve their children's problems. That type of thinking only escalated the violent behavior in these cases because the root cause became buried and ignored by all of the adults involved.

A few teachers used rewards of stickers, charts and candy to control the behavior of the group of children. I must mention that one teacher's actions violated CACFP guidelines. Withholding or rewarding food to children has been a long standing no–no in all schools and regulated centers that are certified under the CACFP.

These outdated tricks for volume control did not work with the children who had severe behavioral problems. A few of the children who had no behavioral problems to begin with were rewarded for good behavior, they refused the rewards.

One student teacher throughout the day used the verbal command— reward and punishment system—reminding children as she announced: "do what I want you to do or you cannot do what you want to do." This teacher was reinforcing her personal signature on the classroom of children. The state's early childhood educational program guidelines do not support or train in this method for disciplining young children.

Another teacher consistently punished one child who could not keep up with the group. The child was shorter than the rest of the children. Almost every teacher adored the child with the exception of the one teacher with the strong hand. She had reinforced her personal signature on this child and others and it was acceptable to the director.

On one occasion a three–year–old who was almost four, was at the top of the list of children in the center whom had serious behavioral problems. Her mother had relinquished all rights of the child to the father when she was an infant. The child was left with a father who would not or could not parent. Extended female relatives and neighbors had taken on the role of caring for the child until it became too much for them. The child was enrolled at the center through a referral. She consistently bit many children and teachers on a daily basis.

One day a senior teacher was standing nearby and immediately asked the child why she had bitten me. The child told the teacher that I had hurt her. The senior teacher in front of all the other children told the child: "well when Cameron hurts you what should you do? Use your words okay." I was professionally stunned that this senior teacher reinforced abuse which never happened using my name in the same sentence in a room full of children. Where and when did this teacher receive her education and training from? This teacher had placed her own personal signature on the children not only in her classroom but on many others at the center as well with the director's full support to do anything she wanted to whether it was right or wrong.

These four teachers and the director at the center had reached coniunctio. This created a new recipe for the center's standard of education, child care and discipline of young children. Other senior lead teachers had learned not to interfere with them.

This type of authoritarian hierarchy system and alliance had been in place and practiced for many years. Change through re–education was unattainable, narcissism and bullying was the dynamic that held them at the top as the winners, and they could do anything they wanted to do whether it was right or wrong in reference to modern educational standards.

To re–educate a director or senior teacher will meet with full resistance when they have been given full–autonomy with no one to answer to but themselves in the academia hierarchy. The attitude of privilege, mastery and authoritarianism to validate one's self importance is what gained dominance in our cultural history. In this case I had walked directly into the core of this cultural phenomenon at this early childhood educational center.

This form of educational and socially learned behavior is introduced at a very young age to children from adults and their environment. The cycle is then repeated over decades and throughout the centuries. The outcome for the grown child will always be the same, an adult whose emotional development needs were never met.

Their innate intelligence and conscience is buried and silenced during their lifetime. Their life goal is to seek self-worth and validation from within the hierarchy as they climb the different levels to a position that gains them access to rights, acceptance and power over others.

Don't Bend the Child

In every regulated child day care there are designated areas called centers where the children go to play and learn. For example, there may be the kitchen center, dress up center, art center, reading center, block center and computer center. These designated areas are called learning centers and are more pronounced in larger facilities. On any given time of the day teachers may close one or more center to the group of children. These rules are applied differently in different states, different regulated centers and in centers with different elective accreditation.

For example, at one child day care center the group of twenty children in the classroom would be divided among the play–learning centers and placed on a fifteen minute timer. When the timer rang the divided groups would be told they had to leave the play–learning center that they were in and rotate on to another one.

At the child day care center that I taught at, the classroom of children never exceeded fifteen in a classroom on a busy day. The children would randomly choose which center they wanted to play in. This is called open–ended play or free play. There was only one exception to this rule. At the computer center for children at age four, two children were the maximum allowed at a time and were monitored on a ten minute timer.

One afternoon in the three–year–old children's room, the student teacher transformed the kitchen center into a pet shop center with stuffed animals. There were six children remaining for pick–up at the end of the day. The student teacher closed all of the other play–learning centers in the room with the exception of the pet shop. She informed the six children that they could only play at her center for the remaining hour and a half. No one was the wiser to her violating early childhood educational program guidelines. She was a bully and had been groomed by the director that she could do anything she wanted to further fueling her narcissism.

She had been employed for almost two years at the center while attending state college. The student teacher had gained pre–eminence in the director's hierarchy of teachers and joined an alliance. As a reward she had gained full–autonomy in her work and a full–time permanent employment position. The director's employment decision re-enforced her bullying of other teachers and children, because she could do whatever she wanted to do with no recourse.

One day an elderly teacher raised her voice as she grabbed the arm of a two–year–old child to scold him. The sound waves echoed and made everyone in the room jump. The director was in attendance, she smiled and ignored the scene. The teacher had seniority and she was allowed that kind of behavior.

Don't Oppress the Spirit

A day at this child day care center involved the processing of high volumes of children. The transitioning was very slow and time consuming. The daily program's order was breakfast, free play, music (singing songs) twice a week, lunch, nap, snack and free play until pick–up by the parent. The initial concept and design of the center's educational program had excellent potential.

The reality was that these children were being told what to feel and what to say by both the center's teachers and director. It is nothing short of adult educators and parents emotionally conditioning a young child instead of nurturing and validating the child's individual feelings and thinking.

For the few children that cried out for parents, when the crying continued up to lunch time, then the center would call the parents. The parent would be asked what they would like the teacher to do with their child? In all of the cases that I witnessed the parents told the teachers to leave their children at the center and to call the parent back after lunch and nap time if their child was still crying. This would equal four plus hours into the day where the child would be physically crying and emotionally overwrought at the same time saying they wanted their mother.

This director and parent behavior results in emotional deprivation for the child. In some of these cases the child's behavior was genuine and in a few it was mimicked. In either case it should never be ignored by the parents.

Parents do not realize how often their child is being pulled, tugged and trampled on during the daily shuffle of going from the playground, to the nap room to the lunch room and so on. The amount of physical and emotional transitioning was very time consuming and demanding in the children's day.

One day a lead teacher withheld a certain food during lunch and at the afternoon snack until the child tried the other food offered first. This action violated the CACFP guidelines and training. The lead teacher was a new hire with a Masters. in Early Childhood Education. She was reinforcing her personal signature on this child and this reflected how she had been taught as a child.

There were up to thirty children in the three–year–old children's nap room. The state regulated nap time is for two hours. Up to an additional forty–five minutes in the nap rooms were needed for processing the high volume of children onto their cots and waking them up to have them put their socks and shoes on.

What is written in the personalized statement of philosophy, mission, and curriculum of a program by a regulated child day care center or early childhood program or preschool, it should be understood by the parents that it is approximately and not exactly what occurs throughout the day. It is a program design written on paper.

In most any center or school there will always be three types of educators and this takes into account the directors and principals – the genuine a.k.a. the real thing, the imitators a.k.a. the frauds, and the scary ones a.k.a. bullies. For any parent they will find it very complicated to differentiate who is who in the educational industry.

Don't Break the Spirit

What becomes at stake is losing one's self or identity when children and teachers are on top of each other in small spaces for long periods of time. What was written under the center's statement in their philosophy's belief was the support and importance of individuality and uniqueness of each child. This philosophy becomes negated when reinforcing to a high volume of children and teachers that there was only good in the group and the group represents the family. The team rules taught were to say what I want to hear, not what you want to say. Feel what I tell you to feel and not what you actually feel. Bad is a bad word and does not exist in the group, team and the center in any capacity or form.

At the end of the day parents were told by teachers that their child had a good day. This did not take into account the crying, fighting, violent incidents, lying, bullying, shaming, denigrating or stealing that had taken place throughout the day to their child while at the center. The fact that a child cried for hours or was hit, bitten or urinated on by another child, was unmentioned unless there was a mark left on the child that demanded an explanation to the parent.

Parents do not want to hear this after a long day at work. Parents are told what they want to hear. The catch phrase he or she "had a good day" was used by teachers to disassociate the parents from their children and it sugar coated the children's experiences and emotions they actually encountered throughout the day.

It must be taken into account that any child day care center is a business with management controls set into place to keep the system operational and permanent. I do not know why teachers or directors would lie to parents. I never have and never would. I do not know if the teachers and director had told the parents the truth what the outcome would have been.

When children hear adults lie about them, how do they process that during their emotional development at a young age? If emotional violence is as harmful as physical violence—why do teachers, directors and parents perpetuate this type of behavior with children in the U.S.? How this country chooses to treat their children is the answer to this question.

Team teaching was defined by the directors as gelling of the two or more teachers in any given room. In the interview process it was explained to me equality incorporated a no hierarchy system of team teaching philosophy and this was expounded upon by the director during my teacher orientation process. Each classroom had a lead teacher and the other team teachers were sometimes called assistant teachers.

Look Inside a Prism

The pan-optic idea in institutions and some businesses means there is a line of power and there's always someone above you and often times below you. Although you may not see you are being watched, you are constantly being watched. There is a hierarchy of power with respect to seniority such as teachers in schools, or managers in business. The longer they are employed the more power and influence they have, in some cases it results in doing the right thing and in others it becomes an accumulation of injustices resulting in ineptness.

A school is another example of a pan-optic idea that separates children by age into different classrooms and the teacher is the person in charge who teaches, gives rewards and deals punishments. The director oversees the teachers and abuse of power, narcissism and bullying becomes achievable not only at the top but also in the links of the chain of command behind the hidden guise of working for the team and forming alliances.

A student teacher, under the director's edict, had seniority over various other teachers. She had taken this literally as did a few of the senior teachers. The student teacher chose her moments carefully. She would attempt to manipulate specific children who had been enrolled in the center for years and whom did not like or warm up to her. She consistently used underhanded approaches with the adults and the young children in the center. In reference to the children, one tool she used was candy to bait and manipulate the children. The other senior teachers who were aware of her character knew enough not to speak up, because it would be futile and would also compromise their place in the hierarchy and their employment.

A fresh new face hired to teach at the center could expect to hear the whispered encrypted warnings from a few of the senior teachers, "never tell them what you think" or "remember the right hand does not know what the left hand does" or "they wear rose colored glasses …they only see the good here and there is no bad." In order to get ahead one had to show faithfulness to the director and the few she kept closest to her while joining their alliance.

The center promoted the idea of all staff being a family. The family belongs to the group where only positive words were allowed. This ideology did not deter a few teachers from forming into factions of their own where they could speak freely amongst themselves. Everyone knows the truth will set you free.

Later I would discover the director had given the edict to all teachers that they were to discipline each other according to seniority based on time or lead positions held at the center. This opened the door for some of the teachers' narcissism and bullying, because they could do whatever they wanted to do. This was one root cause for the anarchy, and abuses at the center. The few teachers who did use abuse of power used it to no end when it came to bullying and ineptitude.

There were intentional strategies to oppress and break one's spirit on a daily basis. For some teachers they learned to cry silently. Daily pain became an accepted emotion inflicted by an authoritarian hierarchy who forbade the truth to be spoken amid the emotional and physical violence.

Teachers at the center suffered not only from the rampant viral and bacterial infections that children carry and pass on to one another which is the norm in all centers and schools. But additionally teachers were commonly plagued with chronic diseases such as cancer, morbid obesity, osteoarthritis, asthma, high blood pressure, migraines and high rates of hormonal problems.

One day a four–year–old inquired whether the word "can't" was a bad word. The child had been told repeatedly by the other teachers, as other children had been told, that she was not allowed to say the word in the center. The girl asked me whether the word "can't" was a bad word. I replied: "No, can't is not a bad word…" Bad was another word that was not allowed to be said, there was no such thing as bad in the center.

Many of the children at the center had two working parents. At the end of the day they were often too tired to watch or discipline their children at home. A few of these parents allowed their children to do whatever they wanted to do while unsupervised. The parent's supervision and interaction with their children was at its all time low after working a full–day.

This was the case for one of the four–year–old boys who consistently had been violent towards other children. At home he was self–inflicting wounds on himself. Both of his parents were working professionals. At the end of the day after pick–up their children were sent to the media game room unsupervised. This had become their family's daily routine. When the center approached the parents on this matter, the parents were in denial that their son's violent behavior was an extension from their home environment and they refused to address the ongoing problems with their son.

At the center some children would return with physical injuries from being unsupervised by their parents. A broken hip, a broken leg, knocked out teeth and torn stitches from a severed chin. These were a few injuries that the children had brought from their home to the center.

The waiting list for enrollment into this high–end center extended itself into the double digits for enrollment into the infants' room and triple digits for the older age children's rooms.

A School

Recognize What It Is

School is a catchword for any place of education. The term school is used by any institution or person offering training or educational services to the public. It may mean a public or nonprofit approved or accredited organizational entity devoted primarily to academics. A school may operate primarily for educational purposes on a full–time basis for a minimum school year and employ a full–time staff of trained instructors. School may also mean a building or structure for the purpose of instruction and a place for the process of learning.

The definition of a school may denote an environment that is equitable, accessible and supportive, secure, safe and supports educational goals in an atmosphere conducive to teaching and learning.

The term home schooled is used when parents provide education in the home. Regulated registered family and group child day care home centers have an educational goal oriented environment and this is mandated by state regulations. However I have never heard a parent or child address these two types of regulated child day care centers as schools. I have repeatedly heard parents and children address licensed child day care centers as schools.

The following is my attempt to demystify the teaching and the learning process of young children. What was once common knowledge to many parents that taught and cared for their children in their home, it is now reintroduced to parents as part of a developmentally appropriate educational program for children enrolled in child day care centers, early childhood programs, preschools and nursery schools.

Blocks

They are learning to experiment with ideas.

They are building fine motor control by gently placing one block on top of another.

They are building hand–eye coordination.

They develop social cooperation when building with friends.

They develop recognition of shapes.

They are introduced to concepts such as balance and gravity.

They develop the skill of classifying when they use their favorite shapes.

They improve their language skills when asked to explain their structure.

Dramatic Play

They use their imagination, language and body.

They are able to recreate situations that they might not understand, and resolve them through play.

They grow in areas of social and emotional development.

They develop collaboration skills, problem solving skills, critical thinking skills and develop literacy skills.

Hands–On Manipulatives

They acquire mathematical concepts such as size, shape, patterning, sorting and matching.

They develop small muscle strength.

They develop sequencing skills.

They develop counting skills.

They develop an understanding of quantity.

They develop an understanding of length and height.

Cooking

They learn to follow directions.

They learn about sequencing.

They stimulate all five senses.

They learn to recognize shapes and colors from different kinds of foods.

They improve their small muscle coordination from using different utensils.

They are exposed to words by way of a recipe.

They learn about other cultures through multicultural recipes.

They learn chemistry by seeing separate ingredients become something else.

They develop self – confidence when they eat what they created.

They learn patience while items are baking or cooking.

Listening to Stories—Looking at Books

They are exposed to reading.

They develop their imaginations.

They will develop a sense of sequence because stories have a beginning, middle and end.

They learn to listen and expand their attention span.

They develop their vocabulary by hearing new words read to them.

They learn about different concepts, people and places.

They're minds are being stimulated, and neural pathways are growing and connecting.

They are seeing that letters make up words, words make up sentences and sentences create stories.

Writing

They are practicing using writing tools (crayons, colored pencils, markers).

They develop an understanding that writing conveys meaning.

They develop their small muscles.

They make up their own stories.

They begin writing their names.

They are developing an enjoyment for something they will do for the rest of their lives.

Music

They learn to appreciate all types of music, including those from other cultures, countries and time periods.

They develop large muscle skills while dancing.

They learn new words from singing songs.

They develop their imagination while listening to music.

They can strengthen their ability to hear the sounds, a skill that will serve to connect sounds with letters.

They learn familiar patterns and the more easily they will recognize them in print.

Art

They develop their creativity.

They learn to make decisions.

They develop self–confidence.

They develop their small muscle skills.

They are able to express themselves.

They develop language skills when they discuss their work.

They learn to trust their decision making ability.

They never have a sense of failure because they are creating something totally original. It cannot be compared to another child's or judged.

They learn to finish projects.

They develop a sense of pride in themselves.

They learn to draw lines and curves—skills that will serve to unite writing cursive, print and numbers.

They learn primary color sets that when combined can make a range of colors, this leads to stimulation of the human visual system by interpreting information about color by processing signals

Listen to the Children

At the private child day care center where I worked there were extracurricular classes. For an additional fee parents could elect to have their children participate in a variety of lessons such as Dance, Music, Spanish and Swimming. The children enrolled into these classes would miss their nap time. This too often resulted in overwrought, exhausted, physically combative, and hysterical crying children for the rest of the afternoon.

On other occasions when walking daily by the different classrooms, a child could be heard crying out for their mother or sometimes for their father. These moments came and went throughout the day. On some occasions the crying never ceased and lead to physical hysteria and the child became ill.

Parents make a common mistake of scheduling a child's part–time enrollment in preschools and centers for every other day. This creates a level of inconsistency and unpredictability for the child because of the changing of caregivers and other children resulting in the child not knowing what to expect from day to day.

Whether the child was enrolled full–time or part–time they would cry in moments of distress at the center. Their grief was due to hurt, exhaustion, anger, fear, separation and anxiety, and/or disorientation when waking up from their nap due from sleeping in an unfamiliar place and the brain chemically altered to protective mode disrupting the natural sleep stages.

The young children's feelings associated with home sickness, loneliness and being left by the parent in the mornings at any center or preschool exist and are authentic.

For example; the class of three–year–old children could not read a clock. Some had learned to tell time by the order of scheduled daily activities. In more than one case a child experienced uncontrollable hysteria and crying. This trigger occurred when the parents did not pick their children up on time according to the scheduled activity. At this vulnerable young age children feel abandonment, rejection and fear from the most important source in their lives, their parents and in most situations from their mother.

Most of the parents at the center gave their children a consistent, safe and nurturing home environment. This provided the children with the capacity to engage in reciprocating relationships with others outside the home. The resulting behaviors include the ability to love, think and play.

The number of children in the center that could not reciprocate in relationships with others had serious behavioral and developmental problems. They came from families that were newly divorced, had a newborn sibling, new step–parent or were ignored altogether in the home by the parent(s). In one of these cases, where there was a newborn sibling, the four–year–old was sent away to stay with the grandparents.

Parent rejection for any child is a genuine emotion and has serious infinite consequences on the family. These challenging children became manipulative, violent and highly confrontational in their relationships with the other children and teachers. Possibly their feelings of total helplessness was a source for their anger. The mimicking of their bad behavior introduced itself to the other children. Once this occurred it was challenging and at times impossible to reverse. This unwelcome behavior spreads like cancer when children or adults are placed in a restricted group on a daily basis.

There is no perfection in child day care centers and early childhood programs or preschools and nursery schools. Perfection can only be a creation of the mind at best. A parent's expectations and their capacity to recognize what choices they have to care, teach and raise their children are individual from one parent to the next and it begins at birth.

It is not only about what or how children are taught but also how children are treated that determines their emotional developmental needs being met and their final outcome in life as they mature into grown adults.

Epilogue

Moving Forward

Changing careers from Early Child Education to Operational Management opened a new door. I would be able to use my corporate and educational training, and experience in managing a departmental staff.

Employment # 1: Within the first year at my new employment and after the honeymoon period ended I asked a co-worker why was 'this' happening? He answered that I should think of it as being in school. Confused I did not understand what he meant and thought that if these types of wrong things occurred at most of the schools that I had attended, it would have met with an immediate call from a parent and swift resolve from the principal. Otherwise someone would be held accountable for negligence and liability and out of a job.

At my new place of employment, the consistent illegal, unethical and mismanagement affected my work as an ops manager for a staff of fifteen. I offered solutions and redirections to the co-owner who was also the on-site manager. My actions met with full resistance. And escalated into one day out of many where I was cornered against a wall in a room alone with the manager, with his face in mine stating, 'he could do anything he wanted to do to me at any time and he could terminate me at that moment if he wanted to'. To further his point, on more than one occasion he ordered me to enter the break room and randomly fire two of my staff for no reason other than he could. I declined. The workplace bullying escalated.

I told the principle owner of my concerns that were occurring on a daily basis. The schemes involved were both financial and human rights violations that targeted my staff the most as they were the easiest to have no confrontation from. All employees experienced wage theft; some were threatened and degraded more than others. He had recruited a few managers to be bullies as well and they easily followed his lead towards certain targets.

When the departmental staff survey that I had designed was completed, the two owners falsified and altered the results. Both publicly announced their doctored results with no conscience in a public forum. Then there were the wage discrepancies. In my case thousands of dollars for paid hours worked could never be recouped because the on-site manager altered the files on my and other individuals' accounts. The principle owner feigned ignorance and any attempt to help resolve the ongoing issues when I brought matters to his attention. Over the course of time he started to consistently and openly let it be known, in front of other employees, that the co-owner could do anything he wanted to do because he owned the business also.

As a supervisor I had the legal right to file a complaint with the EEOC on behalf of my staff. When I mentioned to the government agent that my manager had told me to randomly terminate two employees as part of a harassment game, in addition to others actions, the government agent informed me the owner had the right to tell me to do anything he wanted and I had to comply because he was my manager.

I declined then and will continue to do so when I know it is an illegal or an unethical act when ordered by management to execute. If I had followed that type of order it would make me guilty of doing what is knowingly wrong in the workplace and simultaneously incapacitate my management performance and knowingly result in failure.

The endless denigration, lost wages, violence, sabotaging and lying about my work accomplishments had no end from the owners. Lastly the co-owner created a kangaroo court where I was put on trial before my staff. Next he suspended me without pay for two weeks, falsified performance and evaluation documentation, terminated me and blacklisted me in the tight knit business community. Through his instilling fear daily by means of physical and psychological harassment, he thereby made sure I had no social or business standing.

I never recouped the lost thousands of dollars in earned wages he had deleted in my payroll files. As a former accountant, I took the remaining indisputable evidence of illegal business accounting practices to a government agency. When they performed an audit, the business owners were ordered to pay an estimated one-hundred thousand dollars to the state and employees. The monetary pay out was not covered by their business liability insurance. This settlement came only after the business owners' futile attempt of using attorneys and denying any wrong doing up until the last moment, when the state had finally exhausted all patience with the stand-off and told the owners a trial date was set.

The on-site manager had left a paper trail of stealing monies from various accounts. Furthermore, the human rights violations had been well documented by me for more than a year and a state government agency was accurate and thorough in filing this complaint on my behalf as manager representing my former staff.

In the workplace, bullies in higher management can easily recruit other bullies to form alliances. This was evident when the business owners recruited and groomed two of my former staff to give false testimony to the human rights government investigating officers. The irony was that I fought for their rights and a safer workplace as a group that included them which was represented in the complaint. When I read their false statements, I dropped the case as it would have been futile.

In order to get ahead in this type of work environment, one had to show faithfulness to the co-owner/on-site manager with the result of gained employee privilege. Both owners have the bullying complex that results in the belief they could do whatever they wanted to do, because they could. To establish their own power and importance there can by only one winner resulting in everyone else as the losers.

Employment # 2: I had interviewed twice for this company and the new office building made its way into published articles in top rated corporate magazines.

I was called for an interview and was told at the same time that there was a salary discrepancy on the website listing and was I still interested in coming in for an interview, the wage offered was less than advertised? The interview lasted three hours and the physical work environment was visually spectacular.

On my first day I worked fourteen hours, and the norm became seventy hours a week on salary. During my first week I went to meet the executive manager about ordering new uniforms for my staff because there hadn't been any in inventory for some time and many of the staff had no uniforms. In a belligerent rant and rave the manager told me what he thought of me and it was very negative, belittling and personal in a long winded speech about my professional identity. I sat in his office without any recourse, accept to be polite and remain professional.

At the weekly and daily manager meetings attended by the two executive managers their public humiliation directed at me, occurred in front of all of the managers and it was endless. One manager in particular without fail, harassed me unmercifully, and would make repeated sexual and racist comments. I was not the only victim.

Daily my accomplishments were criticized while the department I operated was understaffed, employees were exploited and not paid or given staff benefits, when it was understood in those circumstances they would be. The departmental budget was doctored when given to the owners.

A supervisor, who was a subordinate to my management position, addressed the departmental staff on a regular basis and confronted them as cows and bitches. Additionally, she openly violated OSHA regulations in the worst possible way. As her manager I asked her to change her behavior and she informed me that she could do whatever she wanted to do because that is who she is. This behavior was reinforced by my manager as she had a long history both personal and business with him whereby they had formed an alliance. He faithfully supported all of her bad behavior under the guise that both had made a pact together. Both vehemently informed me they only trusted each other and no one else in the workplace.

The brutality of the daily harassment from higher management could not be reversed, no matter what I did, it escalated. The mismanagement at the business resulted in many exempt managers working seventy hours a week on salary. These types of employers are a prime example of why President Obama instructed the Department of Labor to update and modify the FLSA coverage for exempt salaried employees under labor law requirements. In simple terms it is called 'wage theft'. The wage amount for exempt salaried employees has not been revised since the minimum wage has changed over the course of the years.

At the end of one day the two executive managers asked me to come into one of the manager's office. My intuition told me that behind the door was an ambush in wait. I turned around from the office's closed door, handed my set of manager's keys to an unsuspecting receptionist. Then I walked through another corridor and handed my manager's radio to security, walked through the front door and never looked back.

Subsequently they did not pay wages for the last week of my employment and my PTO was not honored or paid. Currently to the best of my knowledge I am one of many that experienced sexism and racism, wage 'theft' discrepancies and other labor issues that are a routine practice by the executive managers at this place of business.

Later on I would discover, management employed demotion as a means to an end of not terminating. This sort of business management tactic makes the employee feel socially humiliated and incompetent so they may as well not stay and potentially quit, resulting for the business to avoid paying unemployment.

Employment # 3: My career dream job came true. The hiring manager from the Millennial Generation had informed me they had terminated two people that had been hired by a former manager for the position I was applying for. This was an opportunity for a fresh start at a newly opened business. The department that I would lead was in the beginning stages of an OSHA investigation and was continually receiving very bad reviews on social media. I laid out my business plan to the manager. When I accepted the ops manager's position he literally cried with relief and joy

I implemented Maslow's Hierarchy of Needs for Corporate Management, edited my inherited departmental staff when whoever refused to follow OSHA regulations, or violated the order of operations that I designed and implemented.

I implemented a management practice of validation of job performance based on individualism. This was defined by exhibiting an individual special skill, production based on quantity, quality and volume, behaviorism, and availability. I had zero tolerance for corruption, personal factions and the undermining of management as it would interfere with my business management and time. Often I worked from home after I left for the day as my new manager's office was under construction, as I was told.

The honeymoon period ended when I was blindsided by an assistant manager to my manager who were both Millennial. She and her rotating new hire co-workers would stay out all night clubbing and partying, show up hung over, go into the back office to curl up and sleep in the two executive office chairs forcing me to use the business space where she and her co-workers were assigned to be working. I would email my manager each time she performed these stunts because it directly interfered with my work and time spent at this place of business, and I was on salary.

She recruited the new hires for her department to follow her lead. It included not relaying my business phone messages, physically blocking me from use of the computer or chair, intentionally talking to me while on business calls, sabotaging the order of operations for my department and she took credit for my design and ideas that I was working on with my manager.

It was endless and these types of non-work activities were denied of ever taking place by my manager when I reported them to him. Other co-workers also informed him of what was occurring on a daily basis with this hourly paid mid–level manager when he was not present.

She would disappear for hours at a time while clocked in, to go visit her boyfriend who lived nearby, or leave the property to meet with delivery truck people at her apartment, send co-workers on personnel and shopping errands, and clock in and out for her new muses (co-workers) when they were not on the property. Her position was upgraded with raises and support from the executive managers and owner while retaining an hourly wage which surpassed my salaried wage.

My manager explained to me, that I did not understand how things worked in this environment making a reference to personal favoritism or alliances. He would repeatedly through time tell me that he only trusted her and one other co-worker. I was an ops manager for a staff of thirty, to hear personal confessions from my manager about putting his trust in this bully and her evident incompetence reminded me of Employment # 2. When does the word trust enter the workplace based on personal relations or alliances and not business competence?

Bullies harass and have no empathy. They don't care about anyone but themselves. They have an uncanny ability to not learn or put a full effort into their work or take responsibility for their actions, because of their inherent narcissism. Yet somehow they manage to have every failure and deviant act they generate to not stick and further blame someone else while at the same time taking credit for other people's work. In this bullying workplace environment, bullies recruited other bullies and it started at the executive level management.

After the honeymoon period ended, my Millennial manager became verbally and emotionally violent during our weekly manager's meetings. He took credit for my work, accused me of incredulous assertions of my work from the bulling collective.

My manager continued to refuse to stop the assistant manager and her newest recruit when she upped the ante on the unmerciful harassment and interfering with my work. In a moment, I decided to speak with my manager's manager. The first thing the executive manager said was that it was my fault. That was the beginning of the end when I saw that the red flags were all over this business and the management.

Witnessed continually through an open door would be the business owner ritually going into tirades, criticizing, and blaming failure while dictating absurd business directives to the executive manager. This resulted in a middle age man cowering into a meek physical posture with his head bent and lowered the way a dog is beaten into submission by his master to instill fear. And this cancer spread down the management hierarchy. The executive manager passed it on to my manager and so on.

I decided the only way to continue to do my work was to ignore them. Because they could do anything they wanted to do with no repercussions. At this place of business, they addressed themselves as the family, as the team and they all serve the one. Two co-workers who were Millennial Generation female managers compared the business owner like their fathers and rationalized his dominate violent, 'he is always right even though he was often wrong,' behavior as such so they accepted it as the norm.

My staff of thirty were managed by individualism, individual first and team second and that was our success. There was fairness and no fear instilled to manage my staff. My Millennial manager and the executive managers claimed I was "soft and my staff showed me disrespect." I realized then I was in that same cultural phenomenon depicted in the chapter: "A Child Day Care Center".

The business owner through the management hierarchy in time started using his strong hand methods on my department's ops management design. I was told to cut my staff's hours below thirty hours a week and hire more people in order for him not to pay unemployment. I was ordered to no longer terminate employees but to cut their schedule to two to three days to force them to look for another job to avoid paying unemployment. I was told to offer a lesser wage than what was previously offered to new hires and who were to be eliminated from annual raises.

The owner offered no benefits to my staff. There was a wage discrepancy in the listed advertisement for hiring versus what was actually paid to the new hires in my department when the business first opened which further validated an ongoing pattern of management abuse and exploitation.

As the ops manager I also made the schedules and was told I had to now work six days a week to replace my supporting staff that were hourly paid. What was being dictated to me was fundamentally inhuman and unconstitutional; it is 'wage theft'. These business tactics will have a severe mismanagement backlash in any business.

The owner did not have the education, experience or knowledge in my business field and started interfering, undercutting and destroying the management system I had designed and implemented. If I allowed the owner's new directives to take place, it would fail and reflect on me as the failure.

The social media reviews were excellent for my department for this company. My business community networking had created attention in nominating me for a state employment award. My staff was stabilized and established. The implementation of Maslow's Hierarchy of Needs in corporate management had met with success and the hybrid design of the order of operations was in place. I now informed my manager of my vacation date that was long overdue.

Three weeks before my vacation start date I was nominated and won a state government employment consortium award for my work with the company. Two weeks before my vacation departure date and six weeks before the annual raises, I was terminated from my position under the explanation that they had decided to go in another direction. Three weeks of vacation pay was due, I was given a check for one week on the termination date. A filed invoice for compensation of my car that was used for company business was not reimbursed after numerous requests.

The owner's narcissism was evident in his public boasting and well know verbal script of his multi-million dollar financial success. In an email sent out to all managers the executive manager bragged of working eighty hours one week encouraging team members to not complain when called upon to do the same. This was a red flag. To an experienced business manager, it tells a story of mismanagement. The 'wage theft' through exempt salaried employees and other employees was how the owner made his business profit and became a millionaire.

To instill fear while claiming to own employees is reminiscent of indentured servitude, or bondage. The owner had created the groundwork for the violence, harassment and rewarding incompetence, thereby leading the others to make bullying alliances. This is learned behavior and it becomes very personal in the work environment. The results take its toll and is physically, emotionally, and psychology exhausting.

Everyone knows basic business management 101, that mismanagement drains productivity, time, morale, money and the standard of quality in every facet of a business. Mismanagement consisting of instilling fear supports a bullying network in a business environment and will result in the highest inferiority of production, ineffectiveness and cheating conduct in the workforce.

FINAL CHAPTER

Our innate emotional intelligence has a direct correlation on guiding our thinking and actions. Our society's cultural influences have grown epidemic in terms on how to teach our children not to sense emotion. We must be allowed as children to feel in order to become consciously aware adults. This is a condition influenced by parents, child caregivers and teachers.

To become aware of our actual emotions is imperative as young children in order to be able to have the ability to have empathy towards others when we are adults. Empathy is acknowledgment of other's emotions and validation of feelings. This leads to a form of language translation between individuals in order to be consciously aware of what is taking place with others in the environment.

In nature what is comfort to a child is emotional understanding and intimacy from their parents. It brings with it a sense of safety and acceptance. Once what was a time–honored position in the natural course of how to raise children has now been replaced. Accepted currently as socially necessary is to place children into controlled environments that consist of a high volume of children, child caregivers and teachers. Intimacy, touch, one–on–one bonding and interaction as well as stimulation are negated.

This has resulted in over-medicating, material rewards and the excessive giving of things to children to fill the created void. To witness the lack of conscience in young children is an indication for the immeasurable degree of adults who also lack a conscience from past generations.

These individuals transpire this type of behavior into every facet of life. This includes family, the social environment and the work place. The lack of a conscience in children is groomed at an early age and violent behavior becomes the accepted norm by adults. At a later developmental stage this form of behavior may be introduced or re–enforced with exposure to violent media and addiction to social media in a society that is hyper-competitive, while focused on success with the added ability to tune out when they don't feel like responding.

The lack of empathy on the rise in the U.S. preceded the introduction of violent video games, new technologies and the explicatively violent, culturally racist and extremely misogynistic lyrics in trendy music and media. These forms of media entertainment unlock the floodgates wide open for young people, who had no behavioral problems before, to emulate these types of violent behavior and thinking that is presently socially acceptable.

Words have power, music has energy and media images imprint thought. This has added to the already existing socially violent behavior that has become endemic in this country. To take what they want when they want it because they can is integrated into emotional, physical or sexual violent behavior. Privilege, mastery and conquest, this is what gained dominance in our cultural history from the past centuries.

To teach children not to feel, to disassociate when experiencing emotional deprivation will lead to invalidation of the child. This may be the consequential results—when children raise children, when high volumes of child caregivers and institutions raise children or when children raise themselves because parents totally ignore them.

In our culture it is the standard and accepted practice to perpetually degrade women and children. This type of violent behavior is an unrelenting entitlement that includes abusive dialect aimed at women's bodies, women's significance and worth, women's level of intelligence and innate natural senses.

A little more than fifty years ago women did not have access to birth control or the legal right to an abortion. For more information on the former issue please refer to Author Barbara Seaman's *The Greatest Experiment Ever Performed On Women*. This book takes an in depth investigative study into the birth control industry in America. Ms. Seaman encounters a synergy of government politics in women's health-care and private business—combined with a tremendous amount of deliberate indifference to women's bodies, reproduction, health-care and lives.

When Ms. Seaman first spoke publicly about the pre–existing medical facts on record, she was fired from her job, blacklisted, shunned and threatened in an American culture that did not want the truth to be known. Unprecedented numbers of women from all age groups were rapidly experiencing extremely painfully horrifying deaths directly related to greed, corruption and dominance in the women's health-care industry supported by government administrative agencies.

Going further back into American history, in 1920 the passage of the Nineteenth Amendment to the U.S. Constitution finally gave all women the right to vote. The culturally accepted societal privilege to utilize and humble women is inherited—the old social pattern is repetitive from one era to the next.

This form of degradation in thinking and behavior is formulated in childhood and carried forward into adulthood. This type of violent behavior is a response to the lack of ability to be intimate with others in an equally reciprocating relationship. It is learned behavior rooted in a society that instills fear to dominate and control.

The goals of privilege, mastery and conquest are rooted in our cultural history while at the same time not acknowledging emotional developmental needs of children in this country. All mammals have emotional needs.

Those who are not in touch with their own feelings are not likely to have a sense of conscience. They feel no remorse, no guilt for causing harm to others and it is learned behavior. Painful childhoods may cause a child to feel no pain. They have learned to not feel and have lost their natural ability to develop a sense of conscience. Young children are taught to remain emotionally detached and to disassociate when faced with separation from their main caregiver.

Mothers in particular are told and trained in patriarchal cultures to emotionally, physically and mentally disengage when leaving their children with others to raise and teach. This specific American cultural behavior in parenting, over the past centuries was initiated between the mother and her child at age five–years–old when the child entered kindergarten. Today mothers emotionally and physically surrender their infants, along with disengaging their innate role between mother and child, at the age of six– weeks–old. Regulated child day care centers under state statutes are permitted to enroll children no younger than six–weeks–old unless special written authorization is given to the center through mediating parties.

Three and four–year–old children who develop a lack of conscience are no different than the twenty–year–old or forty–nine–year old adult with a lack of conscience. What they also have in common is violent behavior that includes deviance and manipulation that inflicts pain onto others, to get what they want or to retaliate in order to gain empowerment. It is learned behavior and these human developmental emotional markers will be with these individuals for the rest of their life time.

They do it because they can and that is who they have become. They will be surrounded by business associates, friends and family who will deny the perpetrator has committed any violent act or crime. Their supporter's co–dependency in this type of relationship will personally bind them together and empower them both through the alliance. This pattern of behavior completes the full cycle that will be repeated over and over again as it holds the group together.

The child or adult will be very emotionally needy as these needs were never met in childhood. At the same time, they will be emotionally unavailable while they conspicuously treat others in an emotionally or physically degrading manner. Accordingly, they also lack the ability to love or return love and it will compound this unnatural state of human consciousness. This behavior creates the complete circle of destruction of the self and all of those around them.

Civilizations in the past and now continue to destroy themselves using this identical cultural template in their societies. On behalf of entire civilizations, it is self depreciating and devastating. This form of controlling and manipulating violent behavior will be mimicked by others in most all types of settings. It becomes part of the recognized hierarchy and social order characterized by the leaders and the followers in the group.

The golden rule to treat others as you would want to be treated and to take responsibility to protect others has vanished on the whole. This was the basis of the contemporary model of human rights. The concept is imperative for any society to evolve from its present state of emotional and psychosocial development in the course of human evolution.

The modern system that was put into place to protect human rights has its own set of problems. As violent and corrupt individuals, businesses or governments are brought into the judicial system they plot a course of denial in the company of their attorneys and numerous supporters. Those who protect the perpetrators are rewarded through financial gains and privileged treatment within the hierarchy of the group. These sorts of actions are rooted in their own lack of conscience, low self–esteem and personal alliance within the group. This allows for the never ending cycle of corruption, incompetence and violent behavior in the core of a society's unconscionable spirit.

The numerous judicial systems were created to enforce laws to protect the innocent victims. It is a continual game for the defendants because they have played the game many times before. They know what works and doesn't work in order to win. When they do win, they always go back to committing the same violent behavior and injustices as they did before. This is their psychological profile and that is who they are. They do it because they can. Their supporters help them because the form of empowerment they receive reinforces their need to be part of the social hierarchy of the group. Instilled fear plays a role to become compliant to support the violent behavior in the group.

A higher society will know how to feel, will have empathy, will have a conscience, will raise and teach their children to value their emotions and others. To love and to be loved starts from the moment of birth. To teach children not to be aware through disassociation or to discount their distress contradicts what nature has already revealed over millennium. It is an act against human development and nature, it is emotionally depriving children.

A culture without empathy fuels the everyday violence and corruption into almost every spectrum of their society. It becomes part of the fabric in public and private businesses, governments, religious organizations, health-care institutions, educational systems and everywhere.

This escalation and multiplicity of a society's corrupt spirit takes on the form of bullying as an extension to power over the "all." Bullying has existed for centuries within the global world's framework and it seems to have come to a forefront in our modern day society. It is learned behavior with its roots in very early childhood development when emotional developmental needs are not met.

When spirit and instinct are in harmony, the path to freedom is a process of intuitive transformation. To search for interior knowledge, to understand the universal truths, is to move forward together to participate in a learning experience to co–create and raise consciousness. Learning begins from the time of birth and in the home.

THE STORY BEHIND THE BOOK

The book starts with birth. While acting under color of law a rape occurs. When numerous complaints are filed all of the documents are destroyed by multiple assigned investigative agencies. A quest begins throughout the book to find the answer as to 'why'? This leads into the education and behavior of adults whose professional roles are to teach, uphold laws and serve the community.

Education is decoded and deconstructed for the reader. Explained are the numerous diverse methods, contents and behaviors in educational formats. The book becomes a guide for parents, educators and administrators.

In the Epilogue the reader is brought full circle to the original question 'why'? Education is not only based on what and how we are taught. How we are treated and learn to treat others determines the outcome to break the cycle of violence, and corruption in our daily environments.

BIBLIOGRAPHY

Books

Asher, Donald. *Cool Colleges: For the Hyper–Intelligent, Self–Directed, Late Blooming and Plain Just Different.* Berkeley, CA: Ten Speed Press, 2001.

Carmack, Lisa Jobe. *Philippe in Monet's Garden.* Boston, MA: Museum of Fine Arts, 1998.

Colfax, David & Micki. *Homeschooling for Excellence.* New York: Warner Books, Inc. 1988.

Fiske, Edward B. *The Fiske Guide to Colleges Nineteenth Edition.* Ill: Sourcebooks, Inc. 2002.

Graham, Lanier. *Goddess in Art.* New York: Artabras A Division of Abbeville Publishing Group; First Ed., 1997.

Greenia, Mark. *Energy Dynamics: Conscious Human Evolution; Axioms and Resources for Personal Growth, Balance, and the Evolution of Your Body's Energy.* IN: Unlimited Publishing LLC, 2001.

Hoff, Benjamin. *The Tao of Pooh and The Te of Piglet.* New York: Penguin Books 1994.

Leaf, Munro. *The Story of Ferdinand.* New York: Puffin Books a Division of Penguin Books, 1977.

Maslow, Abraham *Motivation and Personality 2nd ed.* New York: Harper and Row 1970.

Meador, Betty DeShong. *Uncursing The Dark.* New York:Chiron Publications, 1993.

Pilkington, Doris. *Rabbit–Proof Fence*. New York: Miramax Books, 2002.

Seaman, Barbara. *The Greatest Experiment Ever Performed On Women*. New York: Hyperion, 2003.

Stevens. Richard. *Erik Erikson: An Introduction*. New York: St. Martin's Press, 1983.

Wolf, Naomi. *Misconceptions: Truth, Lies, and the Unexpected on the Journey to Motherhood*. New York: Doubleday Publishing, 2003.

Reference Sources and Documents

Child and Adult Care Food Program (CACFP). http://fns.usda.gov/cnd/care/.

Family Educational Rights and Privacy Act (FERPA). http://www2.ed.gov/policy/gen/guid/fpco/ferpa/.

Holt, John. http://www.holtgws.com/.

In The Supreme Court of the United States October Term (1995). *On Petition for A Writ of Certiorari to The United States Court of Appeals for The Second Circuit*. By Cameron Kidston. Document no. 95–6113. D.C., 1995.

Lake, Ricki. *The Business of Being Born,* DVD. Directed by Abby Epstein. Burbank, CA: New Line Home Video, 2008.

Mpeka, Fezela, Theo Sebeko. *Kirikou and the Sorceress,* DVD. Directed by Michel Ocelet. France: Gebeka Films, 1998.

NACCRRA and Child Care Aware and Provider Appreciation Day (PAD). http://NACCRRA.org/.

National Association for the Education of Young Children (NAEYC). http://www.naeyc.org/.

National Association for Family Child Care (NAFCC). http://www.nafcc.org/.

United Way of Buffalo and Erie County. *Education: Success by 6*. 2002. http://uwbec.org/contetn/pages/sby6/.

Book Review

"Thank you for sending me a copy of I Want My Mommy. I really enjoyed reading it. I like the idea of an educational system designed to nurture and protect children as individuals, while helping them grow and develop into adults who challenge racism, sexism and patriarchy. Your vision of an open, nurturing, safe and child–centric educational system is both necessary and timely and your critiques of bureaucratic notions of child care are especially interesting. I was also intrigued by your ideas for a combination of childcare and spirituality. You subtitled the book a "parent's guide," but I think it is equally appropriate, if not more so, for educators and administrators."

Yours,
Barbara Seaman

Barbara Seaman: health activist, Co–Founder The National Women's Health Network and Author of The Greatest Experiment Ever Performed on Women: Exploding the Estrogen Myth.

CPSIA information can be obtained at www.ICGtesting.com
Printed in the USA
BVOW08*0813270816

460136BV00004B/7/P